GOSSIP GAME

AN OUT OF BOUNDS NOVELLA

TRACY SOLHEIM

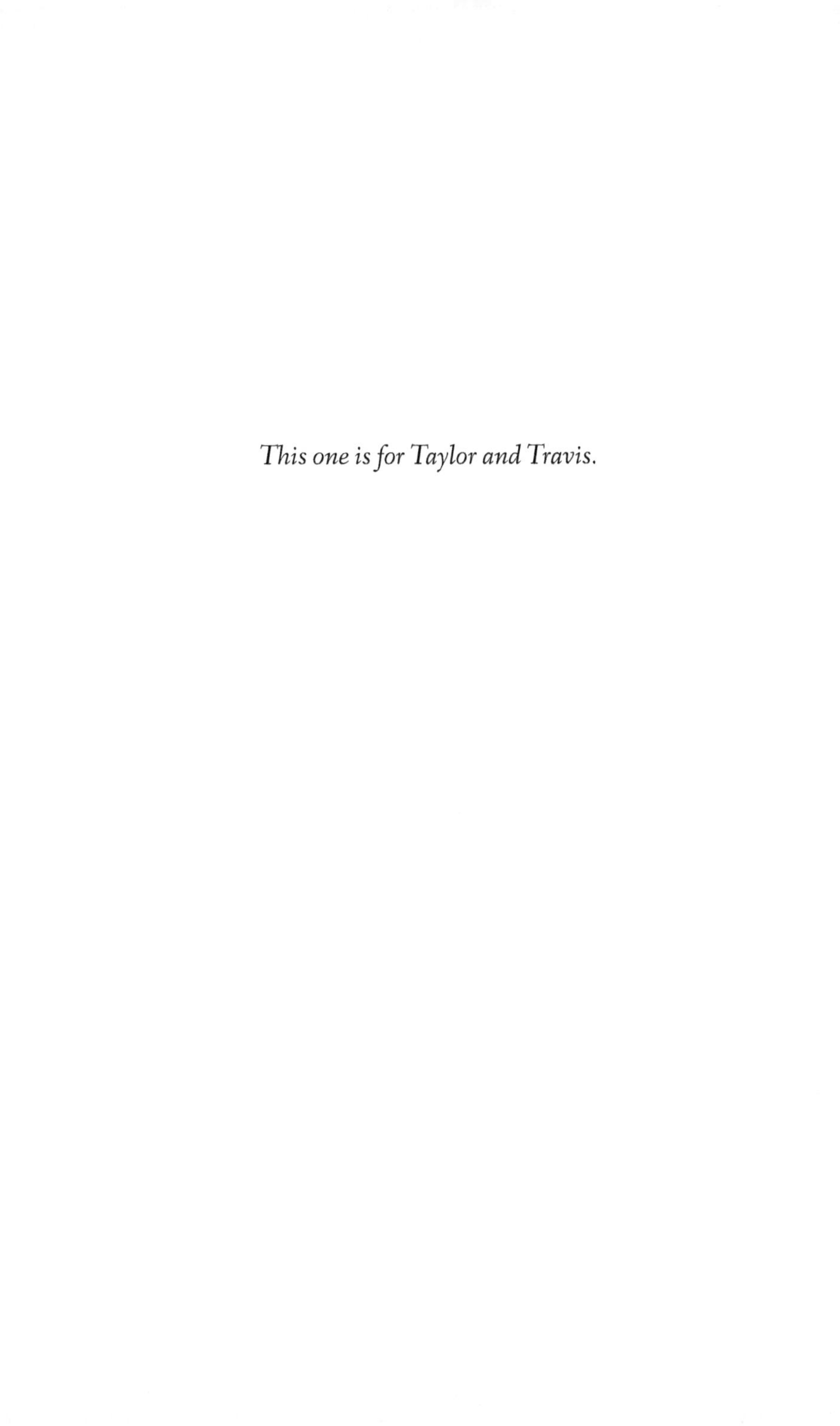

This one is for Taylor and Travis.

ONE

HEADS TURNED as Charlotte Davis strolled into the elementary school's multipurpose room on the arm of her older brother. It had been several years since she'd sucked up the focus of everyone around her when making an entrance. As a spoiled, socialite heiress in her late teens and early twenties, she'd reveled in being the center of attention. Now, however, not so much.

Not that it was easy for either Charlotte or her tall, dark, and handsomely wealthy half-brother, Jay McManus, to fly under the radar. Among his many business holdings, Jay owned the Baltimore Blaze, the football team most of the people gathered at the school tonight likely cheered for. He couldn't go anywhere in the Mid-Atlantic area without being recognized by fans.

As for Charlotte, she'd spent most of her life cursing the fiery red hair that announced her presence like a homing beacon everywhere she went. Coupled with her giraffe-like height—five foot ten without her Louboutin heels—it was hard to make a discreet entrance anywhere. She'd gone to great lengths tonight, however, taming her distinctive hair into a sleek, low ponytail and donning a subdued navy Roberto Cavalli jumpsuit, hoping to blend in.

No such luck, apparently.

While a celebrity at the exclusive private school's kick-off fundraiser probably wasn't uncommon, a notorious tabloid princess among their midst was sure to have tongues wagging in the carpool line come Monday.

Jay nodded as the woman taking their tickets reminded them the silent auction would end soon, with the live auction to begin immediately after. The chatter among the other guests dropped a notch while Charlotte and Jay made their way toward the tables displaying the donated items. She sensed everyone's gaze tracking their progress. Jay stiffened beneath her hold when several of the moms eyed him speculatively. The whispers had doubtless already started in the far corners of the room, guests exchanging theories about where his beautiful wife might be.

She has pink eye, Charlotte wanted to shout. *Likely picked up from one of your precious little snowflakes at sneak peek yesterday.*

She patted his arm as if to say *I got you.*

Jay let out a half-hearted chuckle. "Thanks for being my date tonight, Charlie. Bridgett did a lot of research before we decided to send the twins here for kindergarten." He sighed. "She really wanted to make a good first impression with the other parents. It's important to both of us that Vivi and Gray have as normal an upbringing as possible."

Unlike yours.

He didn't come out and say the words. He didn't have to. They both knew her childhood was anything but normal. Charlotte doubted the private school she had attended on New York City's upper east side even had a PTA. If the school needed something funded, the parents simply stroked another check. No need for charity auctions with catered tacos and free-flowing margarita machines, aimed at loosening inhibitions and opening wallets.

She couldn't fault her brother and Bridgett for wanting their kids to have a stable, grounded life. Growing up under the media's microscope was not something she wished on her worst enemy, much less her niece and nephew. Whatever it took to shield Vivian and Grayson from the trolls of the world, Charlotte was down for it. Nurturing and protecting them had become second nature to her since the start of their lives.

Charlotte reassured Jay with another pat on the arm. "Stop worrying. Those two will be fine."

His gray eyes grew shiny. "Yeah, they will. Thanks to you."

"Don't!" she commanded before glancing around. Only a handful of people were aware that she was the twins' surrogate. And that's exactly the way Charlotte wanted to keep it. Carrying the two babies was her gift to her brother, the person who had been the one constant in her life. And the sister-in-law who made him an even better man.

When the twins were old enough to understand, they'd explain the process of their birth to them. For now, the fewer people who knew, the better. Given how the media treated her, there was no telling how they'd frame the story. For sure not in a way that would make sense to a pair of five-year-olds.

He swallowed roughly, then nodded. "Like I said, I appreciate you stepping in for Bridgett."

"Are you kidding me? I flew halfway around the world just for this moment. It's always been my dream to attend an auction in a room that reeks of smelly gym shoes and fish sticks." She nudged him with her shoulder playfully.

"And here I thought you came home to hire a CEO to manage your company."

Her brother's offhand comment had her enthusiasm for a night out waning. Her cosmetics company, Truly Yours, had grown so quickly that its day-to-day management was becoming overwhelming. Since its inception, Charlotte had been directing the operations. Jay's wife, Bridgett, a brilliant trial attorney, pitched in more and more as the company grew. Without her—and Charlotte's mother—there would be no Truly. But things like supply chain and manufacturing weren't exactly in the attorney's wheelhouse. And Charlotte's education as a jet-setting socialite didn't bring much else to the table. Lately, Truly's investors were becoming a bit more vocal about the company needing someone with business savvy at the helm.

If only bringing in someone else didn't make her feel like such a failure.

She shook her head at her brother's statement, wishing she could stave off her investors the same way. "That could have been done virtually. I haven't been back to the States since Christmas. And I didn't want to miss the twins' first day of school." Which was the truth. She wanted to share in as many important aspects of their lives as Jay and Bridgett would allow.

"Nonetheless, I'm sure there are more exciting things a single woman would rather be doing on a Friday night. Even here in Baltimore."

"It's barely seven-thirty. We've got hours until the club scene heats up. Most of the people going out tonight are likely pre-gaming with a nap."

He shuddered. "Damn. When did I get so ancient? Just the thought of going out anywhere after nine makes me cranky."

"Well, I'll let you in on a little secret." She leaned in. "My bedtime isn't much later. In fact, I haven't been out clubbing in years." Not with a beauty empire threatening to run amok.

He pressed a hand to his chest, his voice mocking. "Say it isn't so? Who are you and what have you done with the impulsive wild child Princess Charlotte?"

She shot her brother a withering look as she slid her arm from his and casually perused the items laid out on the long tables. The paparazzi had dubbed her "Princess Charlotte" when she was fifteen. At first, she adored the ridiculous nickname, steering into the skid and acting out the part of the reckless, pampered heiress to perfection, much to the delight of tabloid editors around the globe.

At least someone was paying attention.

Left out of her father's will, Jay had taken off to parts unknown to lick his wounds and make his own fortune. The grief of burying two husbands sent their scientist mother back into the lab, where she felt more in control of her world. That left Charlotte to navigate the difficult coming of age years while on a very long, gilded leash. It wasn't as if she was neglected physically. She had plenty of money and staff to see to her needs and her wants.

Except her most important one.

Love.

So, she'd traipsed around the world searching for the attention she wasn't getting from her family. It didn't take long for her to find it. Unfortunately, it took a few years longer for her to realize most people were more enamored with her trust fund than with her.

Thankfully, both Jay and their mother found their way back into her life before things got dire. And with Bridgett and the twins, they were a proper family. *Finally.* It was revitalizing to ditch the Princess Charlotte label, and all the ridiculousness that went with it.

Charlotte had spent the last six years quietly remaking herself as a successful businesswoman. She'd tapped into her mother's renowned science brain to start a sustainable cosmetics company aimed at teenage girls. The purpose behind Truly You is to empower young women to love themselves as they are. To choose simple, healthy makeup, but only when needed.

Much to her surprise, the products took off among teens around the world. Young women embraced the idea of healthy skin and "less is more." Charlotte unwittingly found herself as the voice of a new generation of women who wanted to feel free to be themselves—unfiltered—and not constantly aspiring to turn themselves into what they saw in magazines or on social media. They proudly sported the affirmation bracelets Charlotte wore on her own wrist, the simple bands selling out often.

The three simple silver bands served as Charlotte's talisman, grounding her when days got rough. She never took them off. They were a gift from Jay more than a decade earlier. The inscriptions on them reminded her daily not to give up. That she would prevail. Every night, before she closed her eyes, she told herself the life she'd built was enough. That all she needed was her career and her family to fill up her well with love.

Mostly.

She fingered one of the beaded bracelets someone had donated. It looked to be handmade by an artisan just cutting their chops on jewelry design. A student here at Shepard, perhaps. Still, it was lovely. She'd give it to Vivian. "Give me your pen," she demanded of Jay.

Her brother reached into his suit pocket and pulled out his silver Montblanc. He arched an eyebrow as he handed it over.

"What? Isn't it the point of the evening to buy things?" She scribbled her name and a dollar amount on the form.

"Oh my gosh," a female voice gushed behind her.

Charlotte turned around to find a woman clasping her cellphone to her chest.

"My daughter made that. She's in the upper school," the woman said. "She was hoping someone would bid on it. But she'll absolutely freak out when I tell her you did. Both my girls are so inspired by you. They love your lip gloss. And the bracelets, of course."

The woman pointed to the three slim silver bangles Charlotte never took off her wrist. They'd been the inspiration for the affirmation bracelets that were now so popular.

"That's lovely to hear," Charlotte replied. "Please tell your daughter she does beautiful work."

The woman gestured with her cellphone. "Would it be okay if I got a picture of you standing beside it? My girls won't believe me without photo evidence."

Charlotte laughed. "I get it. It didn't happen without the pictures to prove it."

She picked up the beaded bracelet and wrapped it around her wrist before smiling for the camera. The woman snapped the photo, thanking Charlotte profusely.

"You're a wonderful role model for our girls. Especially your message about paying attention in school so they will have the tools to pursue their passions. We moms appreciate them having someone like you for them to look up to."

If only I'd followed my advice and took school more seriously. I wouldn't be handing my company over to someone else to run.

Jay wrapped an arm around Charlotte's waist as the woman made her way back to her table.

"Have I told you how proud I am of you?" her brother, who managed multiple enterprises, murmured.

"At least a million times."

Neither mentioned the irony that a decade earlier, most mothers wouldn't want Charlotte's influence on any of their offspring. Her outrageous clothing—if the flesh-baring outfits she'd paraded around in could even be called that—and rash decisions were well documented by the paparazzi for everyone passing through grocery store checkout lines to see. It was a good thing her days of reckless behavior were behind her.

The lights dimmed, and a woman announced the close of the silent auction. Jay led them to two seats at a table near the back of the room.

"You should have at least put your name on something," she chastised her brother. "Isn't the point to fit in?"

"Relax," he whispered. "The Blaze community relations staff is donating an experience to the live auction."

"Welcome everyone," the woman who had taken their tickets minutes earlier said from the stage. "We have five unique student opportunities tonight for you to bid on. Remember, this is for the children, so don't be stingy."

There were a few groans mixed in with the applause from the crowd as the woman handed the microphone off to the auctioneer.

"First on the docket is the ever-popular Shepard Academy carpool lane street sign," he announced.

A cheer rose, along with the tension in the room, as everyone scooted to the edge of their seats. Charlotte exchanged a "who-knew" look with her brother when the bidding reached nearly two thousand dollars for the chance to have the carpool lane named after their child for a year. That was followed by an opportunity to have the principal dress up as a bumble bee and chauffeur a student around in her yellow VW "punch bug." The good-natured bidding volleyed back and forth throughout the room. The parents were becoming much more animated as the night wore on.

"And for our last experience," the auctioneer announced thirty minutes later. "We owe a special thank you to Jay and Bridgett McManus, parents of rising kindergartners, Vivian and Grayson, for their one-of-a-kind donation." He raised his arm to gesture to a man standing in the wings, waving him onto center stage. "An afternoon of bowling with Blaze quarterback, Noah Hudson."

A chorus of gasps filled the room when the auctioneer was at once dwarfed by six-foot-five feet and two hundred thirty-five pounds of well-honed muscle. Charlotte had long ago memorized his stats from the Blaze website. His sandy hair was neatly combed, except for the perpetual cowlick that always seemed to have several strands standing at attention above his left eye. This far away, it was difficult to read his expression, but she was sure those soulful, dark brown eyes were quickly sizing up the room just like they do on the football field right before he snaps the ball.

Decked out in khakis and a Blaze quarter-zip, Noah gave the crowd a shy head bob and a wave. He wasn't much for words. Charlotte knew that firsthand.

Just as she knew his lips were skilled in activities that didn't involve talking.

"Let's hope 'Dudson' can bowl better than he can pass," a guy behind them shouted.

A few nervous laughs rang out, while most of the audience applauded politely. Beside her, Jay let out a low growl of disgust at the nickname that odious sports podcaster, Bucky Kincaid, had saddled the Blaze quarterback with. Charlotte didn't dare take her eyes off Noah. Other than his shoulders inching up a notch, he took the crowd's reaction in stride.

There had been lots of chatter among the talking heads on sports radio and television about Noah's abilities as a pro quarterback during the off season. Kincaid's voice being the loudest among them. He was always at the forefront of any discussion, questioning whether the second-round draft pick had the mental toughness to make the cut in the league. Especially after sitting five years behind Blaze legend, Shane Devlin. It didn't help matters that the Blaze were three and fourteen last season, Noah's first as the team's starting quarterback. In a town used to winning championships, that sort of record didn't sit well with the fans.

"Let's get the bidding started at one hundred dollars," the auctioneer said.

"That's probably higher than his bowling score," the loudmouth at the back yelled.

Charlotte watched Noah's lips twitch ever-so slightly as he struggled to maintain a relaxed smile. She squirmed in her seat, anxious for the quarterback.

"You couldn't simply donate a case of wine from your vineyard or something?" she hissed at her brother.

"We did," he snapped. "In the silent auction."

"I'll take him for a hundred dollars," a woman at the front offered.

Jay groaned at the obvious double entendre while the crowd tittered.

Another woman waved her napkin and offered two hundred dollars. Suddenly, women throughout the room were bidding on Noah.

Charlotte glared at her brother. "Who thought objectifying one of your players was a good idea?"

"The experience is a damn bowling party with kids. A

way to connect with fans." Jay tugged at the knot in his tie. "His school age fans. I have no idea what these women think they are getting."

With a huff, she pulled her phone from her purse and swiped through social media until she found the video Bucky Kincaid posted yesterday on his site. It was intrusive footage shot by the paparazzi of Noah washing his vintage Bronco, wearing nothing but a pair of skimpy workout shorts. Fifteen seconds of mouthwatering, rippling muscles and damp, sun-kissed skin, before Noah realized he was being filmed and threatened the paps away. Twenty-four hours later, the video had over seven hundred thousand likes and tens of thousands of comments. Most of them women leaving their DM handles.

"This should give you some idea what these women 'think they are getting.'" She slammed the phone down on the table.

Her brother blanched as he watched the video. "Fuck."

The room was buzzing around them, and the bidding climbed to twenty-four hundred dollars.

"Twenty-five?" the auctioneer called. "Do we have twenty-five hundred?"

Charlotte shot from her seat. "Twenty-five!"

"Twenty-five hundred dollars to the lady in the back."

"No," she shouted. "Twenty-five *thousand* dollars."

TWO

"NO! TWENTY-FIVE THOUSAND DOLLARS!"

Noah Hudson slammed his eyes shut, trying his damnedest to keep his cool. The last thing he needed was another viral video, this one of him going off at a bunch of PTA moms.

It'll be a boost for your image, his agent insisted.

Everyone on the team needs to pull their weight with community relations, the Blaze GM had declared.

All you have to do is show up and smile, his coach told him.

They were all fucking morons. This evening had been nothing but a humiliating shit-show since he'd taken the stage.

And that was before *she* opened her mouth.

But, Christ, she had the most spectacular mouth. Full, soft lips that were meant to be kissed. And, oh, the things she could do with that sassy tongue of hers.

He wrenched his eyes open, trying to focus on the fracas in front of him. Anything was safer than thinking about Charlotte Davis. Especially because his reaction to the woman was about to become quite noticeable with him on the stage and everyone else practically at eye level with his crotch.

"This concludes the evening," the auctioneer was saying, raising his voice to be heard over the din growing within the large room. "Thank you all for coming."

"Can she do that?" one woman demanded.

"Yeah. What's the sense of donating something for the kids when you are going to just buy it out from under us?" another woman shouted.

The principal wrenched the microphone away from the auctioneer. "Ladies and gentlemen," she said in her sternest teacher's voice. "Please go ahead to the lobby to pay for your silent auction items. We will announce the final tally from tonight's event on Monday. Good night." She spun on her heel and glared at Noah. "You. Come with me."

Christ. Was he really being commanded to the principal's office?

Since she appeared to be heading in the opposite direction from the parents, Noah decided it behooved him to follow. She led him backstage and down a deserted hallway until they ended up outside the front office. When she punched at the numbers on a keypad, the glass door clicked, and the principal ushered him inside. With a resigned sigh, she plopped down onto one of the leather sofas in the reception area.

"No one has access to this part of the building at this time of night. You're safe here."

Noah bit back a laugh at her comment. He faced down three-hundred-pound linemen every week. No way was he scared of a bunch of over-sexed soccer moms with too much disposable income on their hands. Besides, his reputation couldn't get any lower in this town.

He was counting the days—nine—until the season started.

Then he would show the sports media, Blaze fans, and the football world that he had what it takes to lead the team to the championship. No amount of smack talk was going to force Noah to pack up his helmet and go home. Not even a thirst trap video that asshole Bucky Kincaid invaded Noah's privacy to score.

"Allow me to apologize for the parents tonight," she continued. "I tell them every year to dial it back on the alcohol, but do they listen?" She held up a finger. "Although we'll be able to replace most of the staff's laptops now. I guess we have you to thank for that. Provided Princess Charlotte comes through, that is."

"She will."

The words slipped out of his mouth with the same force and cadence he used when he was calling for the football to be hiked. The principal slowly lifted her eyebrows. Noah could practically see the wheels turning in her mind as she jumped to all the wrong conclusions about him and Charlotte Davis. His defense of her was simply a knee-jerk reaction, that's all. There was nothing between them. A woman like her only toyed with guys like him. She'd made that point crystal clear three years ago.

Time to move this conversation along.

"I'm still willing to host the bowling party." No one in the Blaze front office could say he wasn't doing his part for the team's community relations. "Maybe we can tie it to a charitable campaign? Food banks always need cereal. How 'bout the class that brings in the most boxes in a designated week goes bowling with me?"

The principal tilted her head as she carefully appraised him. Most people assumed, because he was quiet, he was just another dumb jock and the only thing he knew how to do was throw a football. That because he chose his words carefully before he spoke, he was slow. Or, because he was a "hick" from a southern small town with small-town values, he lacked the aptitude to understand the team's playbook.

None of it was true. Not that he really cared what people thought of him. As long as they gave him the football, life was good.

"My mom is an educator," he offered as an explanation.

"Aw," she said with a knowing smile. "I wasn't aware of that. You're a bit of an enigma off the field. I know your dad is a high school football coach, but not much else."

If she was expecting him to give her the lowdown on his life story, she was out of luck. Noah had a hard and fast rule when it came to maintaining his private life: It wouldn't be private if the entire world knew every detail.

The silence stretched until she heaved herself up off the sofa with a sigh. "You followed instructions and parked in the staff lot, I hope?"

He nodded.

After retrieving her bag from her desk, she led him out one of the side doors to the staff parking lot. Her yellow beetle was parked two spots away from Noah's Bronco.

He jerked his chin toward the whimsical excuse for a car. "Nice ride."

She smiled and shrugged. "My midlife-crisis toy." She patted him on the biceps. "Your idea of the cereal drive is a great one. We'll run the contest at the end of the month once everyone is settled back into school. I'll be in touch to set up the details."

Noah reached behind the principal to open the car door for her. "No need for parent chaperones, either. The team will provide them."

Her laugh rang out through the night as she got into the car. "Well played, Mr. Hudson. Well played." She waved at him through the driver's window as the little car sputtered away.

He heaved a relieved sigh while making his way over to his truck. His relief was short-lived, however. As he rounded the hood, he nearly collided with none other than Charlotte Davis, leaning her perfect ass against the side of his Bronco.

It figures.

Noah scanned the parking lot warily.

"Jay has gone home, if that's what you're worried about," she said.

"Your brother doesn't scare me." Nope. It was his potent physical reaction to this woman that gave him the willies.

She stepped away from the truck, the light from the lamppost behind her casting a halo around her head. Noah almost laughed at the incongruity.

"He's not mad at you," she added quietly. "He's—" She made air quotes with her fingers. "—disappointed with the situation."

She huffed out a breath. It was so desolate sounding, it riled up all of Noah's nerve endings. He crossed his arms over his chest, tucking his fingers firmly beneath his armpits, so as not to act on the strong urge to reach out and comfort her. That would be a mistake.

And Noah Hudson never made the same mistake twice.

"Although I'm sure he's pretty pissed at me for making a scene," she continued. "Apparently I haven't quite buried my impulsive nature."

Noah could have told her that three years ago when she'd pretended that he was her date and kissed him senseless in a London elevator. Only to walk away hours later as if they'd never even met, much less touched. He didn't trust his words, though, giving her a noncommittal grunt instead.

Her chin rose slowly as her big blue eyes locked with his.

Hers narrowed. In fact, she was beginning to look a little ticked-off that he wasn't fawning all over her like every other dude in her life.

Too bad.

"Wow," she said, her tone clipped. "Not even a 'thank you, Charlotte?'"

"For what?"

An ugly sound escaped the back of her throat. "For saving your ass back there!"

He scoffed. "My ass didn't need saving, Princess."

Her pique kicked up another notch. He'd obviously hit a nerve with the "princess' remark. Not that he cared.

"Are you kidding me? Surely even you understood what those women were intimating when they were bidding on you?" she retaliated.

Noah absorbed the hit without letting his body react. He wouldn't give her the satisfaction.

"My agent would have taken care of it," he bit out.

"Of course he would have. And that would have given your reputation a boost." Her voice dripped with sarcasm.

"It's not like it's the first time a woman used me as a plaything."

It was a low blow and Noah regretted it the instant the words left his mouth, especially seeing the devastated look on her face.

"I was attempting to pay you back," she snapped. "For London. When you...helped me out of a difficult situation."

Just as he suspected, he had been "the help." A convenient male body when she needed a decoy. Nothing more. It's what he'd figured for years now. Still, it stung to hear her say it out loud. And that feeling pissed him off.

He sucked in a deep breath. "Got it. Your little stunt back there was so we'd somehow be even."

She all but stomped her foot. "You could at least be a little more grateful."

He swallowed the growl threatening to escape his chest. Christ, his mom would be so ashamed of him right now. He was being a total dick. Charlotte and her ilk played by different rules than everyone else. Sure, Noah was a starting quarterback on one of the premier football teams in the US. He didn't earn the money of a superstar—yet. Even when he did, though, he still wouldn't be in Charlotte Davis' league.

Tonight wasn't her fault. She'd obviously believed she was helping by interjecting herself into the auction. Least said, soonest mended, his Meemaw always says. The smart thing to do would be to put them both out of their misery by offering up a gracious thank you and moving on.

He was about to do that when he spied the light of a cell-phone camera pointed in their direction. A few more Looky Lous were clustered behind the man, several of them fumbling with their own phones.

Noah quickly unlocked the door to his truck. "Get in."

"Wow, you really know how to woo a girl." She crossed her arms and cocked her hip defiantly.

This damn woman...

He jerked his chin past her shoulder. She glared at him before turning and spotting the amateur paparazzi. With a softly uttered curse, she hurried into the Bronco and crawled across to the passenger side. Noah climbed in beside her, shoved the key in the ignition, letting the engine roar before peeling out of the parking lot.

Luke Combs was on the radio, appropriately singing about a fast car as Noah sped down the school's long drive-way. He glanced in the rearview mirror. Thankfully, he didn't see anyone behind him. Charlotte turned toward the back window to look for herself.

"It's getting more and more difficult to have a private life," she murmured.

"Tell me something I don't know."

Charlotte groaned, slumping down in her seat. "Bucky Kincaid appears to have made it his life's mission to troll you. And it feels much more vindictive than with other athletes he calls out. I can't help but think it's because of me."

Her tone was contrite, as if—wonder upon wonders—she did feel a minuscule amount of guilt.

"And everything that went down that night," she finished.

Noah stopped at an intersection, sighing as he leaned his head back against the headrest. That was his theory, too. The douchebag sports talk host didn't appreciate being rebuffed by Charlotte. More likely, Kincaid didn't like being tossed over for the nobody second-string quarterback Noah was back then.

Even though Kincaid wasn't a loud voice in sports media at the time, the undrafted former college star managed to worm his way into locker rooms, pestering players for the inside scoop that would help him elevate his status. He'd spent the three seasons since positioning himself as wunderkind podcaster and fan-favorite talking-head on "Football Sunday," the pregame show most of America watched every week. The gig gave him a bigger platform to carry out a grudge.

One that appeared to be entirely focused on tearing Noah down.

THREE

THREE YEARS EARLIER...

It was a typical fall evening in London, chilly with a hint of moisture in the air. The Blaze were in town for a game against the Milwaukee Growlers. The overseas contests were more like a mini-vacation mid-season, with the days leading up to the game a bit more relaxed than other weeks. Mainly because the players and their families were all staying in the same hotel. One evening, Noah had joined several of the single guys for a fierce game of darts in a pub next to the team hotel.

As Noah made his way back from the men's room, he encountered a couple in the dark hallway. The guy had his back to him while he herded the woman against the wall. The hairs on the back of Noah's neck stood up as he drew closer.

"You know you want to," he heard the guy say.

The woman with him didn't sound like she wanted to at all. In fact, it looked like she might be struggling. Noah was debating how he should intercede when she jerked away from the man and launched herself into Noah's arms.

"Babe," she said, her voice a little shaky. "There you are. I hate it when you leave me alone at the bar."

Noah couldn't help but inhale her wildflower scent when she buried her face against his neck.

"Please play along," she whispered. Her breathy request brought goosebumps to his skin. She spoke with an accent that sounded distinctly American. And familiar. But it was difficult to place her while they were in the dark shadows.

After a very brief hesitation—he was a red-blooded male, after all—he wrapped his arms around her waist and pulled her closer. Her soft huff of relief brushed his ear when she relaxed against him.

She was tall. Rarely did a woman's body line up perfectly with his. Noah decided he liked it. He liked it a lot.

"I got you," he murmured.

"Can we go home now?" she asked loudly, presumably for the benefit of their audience.

"Mm-hmm." He was happy to play along with the warm, pliant woman in his arms. It had been several months since his girlfriend had thrown him over for a pro athlete with more zeroes in his contract. Noah hadn't realized how much he'd missed having a female body pressed up against his. Until now. Especially a female body that might be inclined to thank him more profusely later.

She pulled away just far enough to link her fingers with his. Her grip was strong, as if she were hanging on to a life preserver. He gave her hand a reassuring squeeze before she turned to lead them out of the shadows. Unfortunately, the dude she was trying to escape blocked the hallway.

Noah bit back an "oh fuck" at the sight of none other than Bucky Kincaid, a jock sniffing pest who thought he was a bigger talent than he was.

"Well, isn't this cute?" Kincaid sneered. "Does McManus know you're screwing his sister, Hudson?"

The woman next to Noah hissed out a breath. Sure, it had been dark in the hallway, but any idiot associated with the Blaze would have recognized her by her height alone. Noah was a first-class dumbass. One who wasn't going to get lucky tonight.

But he was going to do right by his boss's sister.

"Does McManus know you like to manhandle women in the dark?" he clapped back. Two could play Kincaid's game. "Including his sister?"

She squeezed his hand in apparent appreciation before tugging him toward a side door leading to the service entrance connected to the hotel. The door slammed behind them with Kincaid on the other side of it, thankfully. Noah tried to withdraw his fingers from hers, but she held tight.

"What floor?" She demanded when they made it to the hotel lobby and were lucky enough to grab an empty elevator.

He arched an eyebrow in question.

"I'm not staying here," she explained with an exasperated huff. "I can't very well walk out the front door right now. He's been dogging me all over London."

The idea of that prick harassing any woman had Noah's hackles up. He reached around her and pressed the button for the twenty-first floor. Hiding her in his room for a while wasn't crossing any line, he decided. He rested his hip against the back railing as the elevator doors began to slide closed. They were seconds from a clean getaway when a hand snaked in, pushing the doors apart.

Of course, the hand had to be attached to freaking Kincaid. He stood outside the elevator wearing a smug look. She was right. The man was a wily snake.

Noah didn't think. He simply reacted, pulling Charlotte

against him and covering her mouth with his. It was meant to be a kiss for show. To throw Kincaid off the chase. But seconds after his mouth met hers, Noah realized that the only one being thrown off his axis was him.

That's because Charlotte acted out her part to award-winning perfection. Her supple lips opened without question, giving him access to the sweetness of her mouth. Looping her arms around his neck, she slid her tongue along his with wild abandon. That was all it took for Noah to lose all coherent thought. Suddenly, he was devouring her like some savage just released from captivity.

Not that she appeared to mind. If anything, she acted as if she was enjoying the ruthless way he was kissing her. His body temperature lit up like an inferno when she nipped his bottom lip playfully before soothing it with her tongue. He burrowed beneath her hair to find the graceful curve of her neck, intending to leave his own mark. She tilted her head to give him better access. Her movement brought her body more firmly against his. Christ, she was a perfect fit. A keening sound escaped the back of her mouth when his hands found the curve of her ass, angling her dangerously closer to his growing need.

The unexpected chime of the elevator was like a referee's whistle blowing the play dead. Noah came to his senses first, sucking in a deep breath as he tore his lips from hers. Surprisingly, they were the only two in the elevator, its doors wide open on the fifteenth floor. A mother and her young daughter stood in the hallway looking in, the mother wearing a miffed expression while the child stared open-mouthed at them.

Noah did his best to shield Charlotte from being recognized while he furiously jabbed at the button to close the door. The silence inside the compartment was heavy by the time they arrived at his floor. Now it was Noah gripping

Charlotte's hand like a lifeline as he hurried her through the twists and turns of the hallway leading to his room. Once at his door, he swiped his key card and rushed her inside.

Charlotte didn't say a word. Absently fingering some bracelets on her wrists, she wandered over to the windows overlooking London's Eye, all lit up in the night sky. Noah grabbed two waters from the minibar, downing one in a single gulp before leaving the other one on the desk for her. The cold drink did nothing to quiet his wildly beating pulse, however. He couldn't stay in here alone with her. Not after what just went down in the elevator.

"I'm going to find your brother," he announced. "He needs to know about Kincaid."

She whirled around, her eyes anxious. "Jay isn't arriving until tomorrow. And I'd rather he didn't know about this. I'd almost prefer Kincaid's boorish behavior to Jay in big brother mode." She crossed her arms over her chest and notched up her chin. "Trust me, I plan on avoiding this place for the rest of the team's stay."

Noah's sister was seven years older than him, but he was pretty sure he'd want to know if some asshole was preying on her. He wasn't too keen on keeping Charlotte's secret, either. But her mulish look had him backing down.

"Suit yourself. You're welcome to hide out here." He picked up the Stuart Woods novel he'd been reading and headed for the door. The team's meeting room would be quiet at this time of night.

"You don't have to go," she called after him, her voice still sounding a bit shaky.

Parts of his body argued otherwise. As it was, he didn't think he'd be able to sleep in this room tonight after seeing her so close to the king-sized bed. Not to mention the fact that his body was still humming from their close encounter in the elevator.

Christ, he was no better than Kincaid.

He made the mistake of looking into her beseeching blue eyes and he was a goner. His feet felt like they were frozen to the carpet as he watched her move around his room. She nervously fingered the travel backgammon set on the coffee table. Noah and the Blaze's punter had a long running competition going. Her soft smile nearly knocked the breath from his lungs when she looked up at him.

"I haven't played this in forever." She eased herself down onto the sofa. "Jay taught me when I was in the first grade. Before he...left." Her shoulders slumped briefly. She shook her head as if to wipe away a bad memory before lifting her gaze to him, nearly taking him out at the knees with her impish smile. "The last time we played together, he accused me of cheating."

Noah snorted.

She pinned him with an affronted gaze. "I was nine. And I don't cheat."

He might have believed her had those luscious lips of hers not twitched slightly. Her long fingers made quick work of setting up the pieces on the board before she arched an eyebrow at him in challenge. His head told him to get the heck out of Dodge. Too bad that wasn't the head he was listening to. Noah slumped down into the chair across from her.

Charlotte chattered endlessly about anything and everything while they played. Everything except that kiss, thank Christ. He let her keep score, mostly because her unique scent had scattered his concentration. They raided the mini bar for a midnight snack, neither of them mentioning that Kincaid was probably long gone by now. She was content to stay put, filling the night with her tales of her new business adventure.

If anyone had told him he'd be spending two hours engaged in a conversation about cosmetics, he'd tell them they were crazy. Yet here he was, hanging onto her every word. He sensed he was getting an inside look at the real Princess Charlotte. And unless she had multiple personalities, she was nothing like the tabloids depicted. And everything like a woman he'd like to know better.

By the time she stretched out on the bed and began scrolling through the guide on the television, Noah trusted his libido enough to join her.

"Ohmigosh," she cried. "*Thirteen Going on Thirty*. This is my favorite movie. Have you seen it?"

Noah shook his head despite the fact it was his mother's favorite, too, and he'd seen it more than a dozen times.

"It's more of a chick flick. If you don't like it, we can switch to the Marvel movie."

That wasn't going to happen. He didn't dare do anything to dampen her joy. Instead, he curled his arm behind his head, crossed his ankles, and relished her delight in the movie. It was pretty damn special.

Until he woke up the next morning to find her gone without so much as a thank you note. It was as if she'd never been there. Not only that, but every time he'd seen her since, she'd looked right through him as though they'd never met.

"DO you ever wonder why he didn't say anything? Spread rumors about me? And you?"

Her softly uttered words brought Noah back to the here and now. She was forgetting Kincaid did spill a lot of shit about him. Most of it untrue. But the podcast host was careful with his career. A man would have to be made out of Teflon to cross Jay McManus. And badmouthing McManus' sister would be committing career suicide.

"He's too busy trashing my play," Noah said. He put his foot on the gas and drove toward the lights of the Inner Harbor.

"Puh-lease. Anyone who knows anything about football knows not to lay the blame for last season at your feet. You can't help it if the receivers drop every ball you throw their way."

His lips twitched at the ferocity with which she defended him. One of the things he'd enjoyed during that fateful night was her astuteness about the game. They'd talked into the wee hours about football, among other things, and he liked that he didn't have to explain every nuance to her.

She was only half right about their crappy season not being his fault, however. The quarterback was the undisputed leader of the team. Last year, the offense hadn't been in sync. And that was on Noah. They'd jelled during spring OTA's and training camp, though. And this year was going to be a whole hell of a lot different than last.

"Kincaid won't have anything negative to say about my play this season."

Feeling the weight of her stare, he shifted his gaze toward her. The soft smile she wore hit him squarely in the solar plexus.

"That's the spirit," she said.

He forced his eyes back onto the road, steering his truck onto the circular drive of the apartment building where Jay McManus and his family lived in the penthouse. His boast lost a little of its steam when he saw the swarm of people with cameras awaiting their arrival. Kincaid would have a boatload of ammunition if he chose to use it.

Noah swore just as Charlotte gulped out a squeak.

"Can you turn this thing around?"

It was too late for that. The bottom feeders were already racing toward them.

"This truck isn't that agile."

"Dammit!" she cried. "This is what I get for seeking you out."

That was it. She was on her own.

"Why don't you have security detail like every other entitled socialite?" he snapped back as he pulled his prized truck up to the lobby doors.

Her eyes went round, and her lips flapped open and closed, but no words came out. *Good.*

"Don't. Move," he commanded before getting out of the truck.

Noah ignored the cellphones, the cameras, and the shouted questions as he rounded the hood. Luckily, the building's doorman was the size of an offensive lineman. The guy was able to hold the blood suckers back with his out-stretched arms.

Charlotte kept her face expressionless when Noah opened her door, but he could feel the anger rolling off her. As if all of this was somehow his fault. Or that she would be the one denigrated by the media tomorrow. The woman was impossible. The sooner Noah got her inside and out of his life, the better.

He gripped her elbow to help her down from the cab. A jolt raced up his arm as soon as his fingers touched her bare skin. Her sharp intake of breath brushed past his neck. She stumbled and Noah snaked his arm around her waist, drawing her into his body. Camera flashes lit up the walkway.

"I've got it from here," she murmured once they'd reached the door.

She started to pull away, but Noah held her fast.

"Now who is being ungrateful?" he murmured.

It was rare that he could meet a woman's gaze head on. And Charlotte's was a mixture of wariness and passion.

Christ.

"Goodnight, Princess."

Noah didn't give her the chance to respond, his mouth crashing down on hers. He half expected her to stomp one of her stiletto heels into his foot. He certainly deserved it.

But this woman never did what he expected. Instead, she sighed, allowing him to coax her lips open. He rushed into the velvety softness before she changed her mind.

She tasted like the best bad decision he'd ever made.

Her palms skirted down his back, practically branding his skin through his clothing. Damn this woman. She was going to make him lose his mind. Right here in front of a horde of cameras documenting his insanity. A soft moan of protest escaped her lips when he broke the kiss. Noah took it as a victory.

He gently turned her around and pointed her to the door being held open by one of the building's staff. Pressing his palm to her lower back, he propelled her forward. But not before leaving her with a parting shot.

"Now we are even."

FOUR

SLEEP ELUDED CHARLOTTE THAT NIGHT. Every time she went to close her eyes, she ended up reliving that kiss until she was a sweaty ball tangled up in the sheets. Inevitably, the tears would follow. Her reaction to Noah hadn't waned since that long-ago night in London.

Three years earlier...

"Damn that insipid creep," Charlotte muttered beneath her breath.

She'd come to the team hotel to catch up with Sophie Osbourn, the daughter of the Blaze general manager, and the lead designer for Truly's jewelry. Thanks to Charlotte's jam-packed schedule promoting her brand throughout Europe, coupled with Sophie's rigorous academic demands as a design student, their brain-storming sessions mostly took place via Zoom. Luckily, the team's London game coincided with Sophie's fall break, allowing the two women to spend the day creating together in person. It had been a productive session and Charlotte was looking forward to spending the next two days wandering the London Gemstone Mart with

Sophie as they put the finishing touches to next summer's collection.

If only she could lose the pest who kept popping up every place she'd been all week.

Shame on her for being nice to anyone in the media. But the reputation of the Blaze was important to Jay. And Jay was important to Charlotte. So, after repeated requests, she'd allowed Bucky Kincaid to buy her a drink at an after party following the Blaze's championship win last season. Like most men who sought her out, he thought her politeness entitled him to something more.

Not surprisingly, he was staked out in the lobby when she and Sophie finished up. There would be no polite way to avoid him if she left through the front door. Instead, she'd ducked into the pub next to the hotel, hoping to slip out to the street that way. If only she hadn't stopped to say hi to a few of the Blaze players playing darts.

Her hesitation gave Bucky enough time to follow her. He arrived at the players' table with his trademark insolent swagger, offering up a round of drinks to the guys without taking his eyes off Charlotte. Something in his haughty gaze made her shiver.

"If you'll excuse me, I'm off to the loo," she announced to no one in particular. She'd once used a service entrance there as an escape route. It would work again today. Bucky was quickly on her heels, however.

"It's dark back there. I'll escort you."

Was this guy for real?

Time to nip this in the bud. It wasn't like Bucky was some bigshot in sports media who could torch the team in the public eye. He was just a wannabe jock, trying to worm himself into pro sports by any means necessary. Except he would not be going through her to elevate his status.

Charlotte stopped short of the ladies' room. Bucky moved to hem her in. She gritted her teeth, cursing herself for not calling for her security team to escort her the two blocks back to her flat. Jay would be furious at her. But, dammit, she enjoyed living like a normal woman now and then.

Besides, she could handle this creep. She jerked her shoulders back, so she was practically looking down at him.

"I can manage going to the restroom by myself, Bucky." It was a challenge to keep her tone civil. "Been doing it for years."

He eased his body away, but not far enough. She still had her back pressed against the wall.

"It's just that you've been avoiding me. I was hoping to grab a drink and catch up," he said.

Charlotte sighed. Clearly, she was going to have to spell it out for him. "I don't think that's going to happen. I've got a busy schedule this week. In fact, I have plans for the evening and I really need to get going."

She inched forward, but Bucky didn't budge. Charlotte thought he might have growled. It was dark in the hallway, and she couldn't quite make out his expression. Judging by the grip he had on her elbow, he wasn't pleased about being turned down.

When will I learn to be a better judge of a man's character?

Her pulse began to pound so loudly it was hard to think. Fortunately, her panic eased when she spotted one of the Blaze players, the backup quarterback, illuminated by a shaft of light as he exited the men's room behind them. Charlotte had never met the guy. Not that it mattered right now. Noah Hudson was the lesser of two evils.

She hoped.

"Just one drink." Bucky's words didn't sound like a request. "You know you want to."

That. Was. It.

She jerked her arm free, surprising Bucky enough to throw him off balance, and allowing her to shove past him. Right into the arms of one of her brother's football players. Noah let out a grunt of surprise when she slammed into the solid wall that was his chest. He smelled like soap and hops.

And safety.

"Babe," she improvised, angry that her voice wasn't as steady as she would have liked. "There you are. I hate it when you leave me alone at the bar." She maneuvered her mouth close to his ear and whispered. "Please play along."

After a moment's hesitation, he wrapped his arms around her waist, seeming to be careful where he placed his fingers. She arced into the shelter of his body with a sigh of relief.

"I got you," he murmured.

And he did. Even though he was holding her modestly, she could sense his readiness to throw down in her defense, if necessary. His demeanor was a balm to her panicked nerves.

"Can we go home now?" she asked loudly, hoping Bucky would get the message and disappear. She didn't want to drag Noah into this any further than she already had.

"Mm-hmm," he replied.

He gave her hand a reassuring squeeze when she laced her fingers with his. She said a silent prayer that the hallway would be empty when they turned, but no such luck. Bucky was right where she'd left him, arms crossed over his chest and his feet spread wide like the troll overseeing the bridge in Billy Goat's Gruff.

"Well, isn't this cute?" Bucky's tone implied he didn't think it was cute at all. "Does McManus know you're screwing his sister, Hudson?"

A startled breath escaped Charlotte's mouth. Shit. Guilt washed over her at involving the chivalrous guy beside her.

And the last thing either of them needed was Jay intervening. Before she could voice a retort, Noah beat her to it.

"Does McManus know you like to manhandle women in the dark?" His tone was lethal, nothing like the shy guy he was made out to be. "Including his sister?"

Touché, she wanted to yell. She squeezed his hand instead. Then she dodged to the side of the hallway and through the emergency exit door with Noah in tow. Bucky didn't follow, but that didn't mean he wouldn't simply slip through the bar and back into the hotel lobby to cut them off. They needed to hurry.

Noah tried to let go of her hand, but she held fast. They weren't out of this yet. Besides, having him near settled her ricocheting nerves.

One of the elevators opened its doors just as they arrived. She tugged him into it, relieved it was empty. The fewer people who witnessed his involvement in this little drama, the better.

"What floor?" she asked.

Noah arched an eyebrow, but didn't answer. *Great.* Apparently, he was done playing Boy Scout.

"I'm not staying here," she told him. "I can't very well walk out the front door right now. He's been dogging me all over London."

His face hardened with her revelation about Bucky. He reached around her and pressed the button for the twenty-first floor. She was about to let out a sigh of relief when Bucky suddenly showed up, forcing the doors back open with his hand.

Charlotte froze.

And just as suddenly, she was melting beneath the carnal power of Noah's kiss. Before she could think twice, she was in his arms, her body fitting perfectly against all that warm muscle. She didn't even think to resist—mostly because she wasn't thinking. She was simply feeling. And, damn, did Noah's lips feel good.

Charlotte had kissed more than a few men in her twenty-seven years. She'd never been kissed like this, though, that was for sure. Noah may be quiet and unassuming, but his kiss. . . his kiss was nothing short of an erotic adventure.

His tongue swept into her mouth, daring hers to play along. Never one to turn away from a challenge, she was only too happy to oblige. Especially since this was the most action her lips had seen in—well, a while.

It was as if her body was on autopilot, sliding provocatively against his while their tongues dueled. What started as a chivalrous gesture to save her had morphed into a sensual mating of their mouths. He kissed her like a man on a mission. A mission to pleasure her thoroughly. And, oh, was she down for that.

His hands began to roam over her body, leaving a trail of heat wherever they went. She nipped at his lip, beseeching him not to stop. Not to let go. Ever.

She let out a whine of protest when he abruptly pulled his lips away. The elevator had stopped. More importantly, they were the only two people inside. She vaguely noticed the doors opening and Noah punching at the button agitatedly. Her breathing was a bit fractured as they climbed the remaining floors. Unable to shake off the sensual haze brought on by that kiss, she blindly followed him to his room. Once there, she hurried to the window, threading her fingers through her affirmation bracelets, trying to reclaim her composure.

"I'm going to find your brother," he announced behind her. "He needs to know about Kincaid."

No!

The last thing either of them needed was her brother getting involved. Not when it had taken several years for her to live down what Jay considered her poor choices in men. He would think she'd sought out Bucky's attention on purpose. Not only that, but she didn't want Noah somehow becoming collateral damage in her brother's eyes. Not when she gave him no choice but to help her.

She spun around quickly to stop him. "Jay isn't arriving until tomorrow. And I'd rather he didn't know about this. I'd almost prefer Kincaid's boorish behavior to Jay in big brother mode." That was a lie. But she needed to brazen this out. It was for Noah's own good. She crossed her arms over her chest and notched up her chin. "Trust me, I plan on avoiding this place for the rest of the team's stay."

An expression she couldn't decipher flashed in his knowing eyes before he quickly shuttered it.

"Suit yourself. You're welcome to hide out here." He picked up a book from the end of the bed and headed for the door.

"You don't have to go," she called after him, ashamed that she couldn't quell the panic lingering in her voice, but relieved she was able to bite back the rest of her thoughts.

Please don't go. I don't want to be alone.

He remained where he was, which she took as a good sign. She wandered nervously about the room, searching for the words to thank him for his help earlier. Except it was hard to know where to begin without mentioning that mind-blowing kiss.

Her cheeks grew warm with embarrassment. The intensity of her response had been over the top. He'd only been playing the role she'd thrust him into. Yet, she'd acted like a woman who hadn't seen any action for years. It was true, she hadn't. That didn't mean she couldn't have played it a lot more chill, however. He'd likely chalked it up to her Princess Charlotte reputation of churning through lovers. Her face burned hotter at the thought.

She spied a travel backgammon set on the coffee table, moving closer to sweep her fingers over it.

"I haven't played this in forever." She settled onto the sofa to give her shaky legs a break. "Jay taught me when I was in the first grade. Before he...left."

Before he deserted me.

That wasn't fair. Charlotte's father had done a number on Jay. Hindsight was twenty-twenty, and she suspected that her dad resented the closeness between his daughter and the son his wife brought to their marriage. That's likely why her dad made the choices he had.

And while Jay wasn't physically in the same place as Charlotte, he had always been there for her whenever she needed him. Even when she was a rebellious brat. Which, she was ashamed to admit, was often during those teenage years.

She shook her head at her ridiculousness and looked up at Noah. "The last time we played together, he accused me of cheating."

Noah snorted.

Excuse me?

"I was nine," she argued. "And I don't cheat."

At least not anymore.

She set up the pieces on the board before arching an eyebrow at him, hoping he'd stay. A long moment later, he tossed the book back onto the bed and sat down in the chair across from her. Her stomach did a little victory dance while the rest of her body began to relax.

Charlotte filled the hours, chatting nervously. All the better to avoid the elephant in the room. Noah listened patiently as she jabbered on, nodding, and laughing where appropriate. It was refreshing to be around a guy whose ego didn't demand to own the conversation. He was easygoing with a depth he kept hidden for some reason, only showing it to her when they landed on the topic of education.

And football.

They'd somehow ended up watching her favorite movie, both of them on the same bed. She never once felt uncomfortable or threatened. She was so cozy, in fact, she ended up falling asleep, only to awaken just before six, with his arm draped loosely over her waist.

The sense of contentment was so unexpected it brought tears to her eyes. This was what a genuine relationship might feel like. This was the feeling she'd been searching for all these years.

Except this wasn't the way she wanted to start a relationship. Not when she'd trapped Noah into helping her. Sure, he was the first guy she'd felt secure enough to let down her guard with in a long time, if ever. And he'd laughed and debated with her most of the night. But what if he was just being nice?

Her insecurities quickly snuffed out much of the serenity she was feeling, and her best friend, anxiety, set in. She needed to hurry out of Noah's room to avoid any sort of walk of shame. No way did she want to saddle him with that kind of gossip. Not to mention the potential wrath of her brother.

The Blaze players were moving to a different hotel today so they could focus their attention on preparing for Sunday's game. Charlotte would sneak away this morning and come back in a few hours. If she timed it right, she could catch Noah before the buses left and thank him for his help. Maybe with a few of those scones from the corner bakery he mentioned last night. That would be a nice gesture. One that a friend would make to another friend. She was surprised at how much she wanted Noah Hudson as a friend.

If not more.

He groaned softly, but didn't wake when she slipped from beneath his arm. She gathered up her stuff and tip-toed from the room, thanking the powers that be for an empty hallway and elevator. Three hours later, she made her way back to the hotel, security in tow this time, with the scones and a rehearsed thank-you speech.

"Are those for me?" Sophie asked, startling Charlotte.

All her thoughts this morning had been so centered on Noah that she'd forgotten about the gem show today.

"No," Charlotte hedged. "They're a thank-you gift for a friend." She glanced around the lobby, a lick of panic jumping up her spine. "Has the team left yet?"

"Nope." Sophie gestured in the direction of the ballrooms. "They are finishing up their morning meeting."

"Great. Just let me drop these off and we can head out."

The meeting was breaking up, and the players were milling about, gathering up their luggage before heading to the buses. Charlotte spotted Noah on the other side of the large room. Rather than call attention to herself by cutting through the crowd, she stepped back into the hallway and hurried to the door closest to where Noah stood. He was talking with two of his teammates when she peeked in through the partially open door.

"Where'd you get off to last night?" one of them asked. "You had the high score in darts, but then you vanished."

"Collins said he saw him getting hot and heavy with some woman in an elevator," the other one said.

"Whoa, ho!" The first guy slapped Noah on the back. "What do I always say? Ya gotta watch the quiet ones. QB Two is a playa after all. Is there going to be a round two?"

Noah shook his head. "No chance."

"Dude, I'm sure you can get her a room at the hotel."

He gave his head another shake. "She's not worth the effort."

Charlotte bit back a gasp at the ferocity of his tone.

His teammates groaned.

"Too vanilla in bed, huh?" one of them said.

Noah settled the strap of his carryon onto his shoulder. "Turns out she's not my type. Not even close." The bitter way he said the words rattled her.

As the trio of players headed away from where Charlotte was hiding behind the door, she stood frozen, mortified by what she'd overheard. Had the entire night been all an act? She'd honestly believed he was being real with her. Clearly not. The sting to her pride brought on by his words made her woozy.

She's not worth the effort. She's not my type. Not even close.

Of course she wasn't. She was nobody's type, apparently. And she really couldn't blame Noah. She'd forced him into the charade. A charade that, from the tone of his voice, he very much wanted to put behind him.

So much for being friends.

Or anything else.

The least she could do was follow his lead and stay out of his life. Gulping a sigh, she tossed the scones she'd brought for him into the nearby trash can. She was grateful to have found out about Noah when she did. Thanking him—especially in front of his teammates—would have been a bad idea. If he wanted to pretend as if nothing happened, she could, too. She'd make do with being grateful from afar.

But that didn't mean she'd like it. She ducked into the

ladies' room for a quick cry before meeting up with Sophie. After that, she'd simply forget all about Noah Hudson.

———

CHARLOTTE WOKE WITH A START. Light was peeking in through the cracks in the mini blinds. *Morning, thank God.*

Her road trip down Memory Lane was finally over. Turns out, no matter how hard she tried, forgetting about Noah Hudson wasn't in the cards. And now that she had a second kiss to torture herself with by replaying it over and over in her mind, erasing him from her conscience wouldn't be any easier this time around.

Except she had survived it once. And she would again. It was Charlotte's custom to begin each new day with an affirmation. Something she could manifest into being. And today's was an easy one.

So what if Noah Hudson had the ability to stir up her emotions three years after they'd met? That didn't mean she had to let him. This trip to the States was about seeing the twins off to school for the first time. And working with Bridgett to find a CEO. Panty-melting kisses from quarterbacks had no place on Charlotte's agenda.

With that resolved, she tossed back the covers and swung her legs out of bed. She bit back a shriek at the sight of the twins standing eerily silent in the doorway. Those two were never quiet. Unless they were sleeping. And since they were both dressed for the day, she doubted they were sleepwalking. Seeing these two, hearty and whole, had all the tension brought on by dreams of Noah evaporating instantly. These two adorable faces always had that effect on her.

They looked so much like their parents. It was uncanny. Except for the fact that Vivian had inherited her father's dark hair and icy blue eyes, while Grayson mirrored his mother with blond hair and silver eyes. They both had the same silly sense of humor, however. Charlotte liked to think they got that from her.

Too bad neither was looking very silly this morning. In fact, they looked like they'd both swallowed a bug.

"Good morning, my little chickadees," Charlotte practically sang.

Vivian's bottom lip curled into a pout as she clutched her stuffed dalmatian closer to her body. Grayson puffed out his chest. Charlotte's stomach rolled. Something was not right here.

She dropped down to her haunches and reached out for the twins. "What's wrong? You guys are scaring me this morning." They were both stiff as boards in her embrace. "Okay, did someone eat the last donut? I won't be mad. I'll buy more."

They pulled away and Charlotte thought her heart might shatter. Obviously, whatever had them so solemn was more serious than chocolate frosted donuts with sprinkles.

"Are you going to marry Noah Hudson, Aunt Charlie?" Gray asked.

Charlotte almost choked on her own saliva. "I'm sorry? What?" She glanced between their stoic faces. "Whatever gave you that idea?"

"It's on the TV," he replied. "Mommy and Daddy were arguing about it."

Shit.

Her butt hit the floor with a hard thump.

This cannot be happening.

"Vivi is mad because she wants to marry him," her nephew continued.

Charlotte might have laughed at the idea if she wasn't so disappointed that neither of them would ever marry Noah. She cupped her niece's cheek.

"Oh, sweet girl. He's a very good choice for your first crush." She was surprised at the ache in her heart those words brought on. "But not everything you see on TV is true. We're just friends," she lied.

Vivian sank down into Charlotte's lap, her eyes a touch brighter and her sulk fading. Charlotte wrapped her arms around the little girl, glad that she could make her happy so easily. Yet sad that Vivi would likely have her heart broken by Noah and countless other males in her life.

"Then I guess you should explain that to Daddy," Gray was saying. "Because he said Noah better be ready to clean out his locker today."

Vivian let out an ear-piercing wail. It was all Charlotte could do not to join in.

FIVE

FOR THE SECOND time in as many days, Noah found himself in the principal's office. Except this principal's office belonged to the owner of the Blaze. And the mood was much less hospitable than last night's. He had to work to play it cool beneath Mr. McManus' seething glare.

He returned the other man's stare without blinking. McManus was the dark and broody sibling, whereas Charlotte was breezy and open. Besides their height, the only physical resemblance between brother and sister was their blue eyes—which weren't even that similar in color. Charlotte's were bright and daring, like the center of a flame, while her brother's pupils were pale and cold.

Upon further inspection, Noah noticed their mouths were alike. Both had ridiculously full lips.

Christ!

Noah had to stop thinking about that damn woman's mouth. It was driving him so nutty that now he was checking out men's lips. He was grateful to be dressed in his practice gear of shorts and a Blaze T-shirt, because despite his boss' chilly demeanor, Noah was getting hot under the collar.

There was nothing he detested more than wasting valuable practice time. Especially this close to opening day. He was lucky most of the receiving corps had shown up on a Saturday. If this little inquisition took much longer, they'd all be gone by the time he returned to the practice field.

"I have some questions about last night." McManus tapped his silver pen against his palm, evoking the image of an old-school teacher with his disciplinary ruler.

It didn't rattle Noah. Instead, he concentrated on breathing, letting the silence stretch. He'd learned early on that nothing good ever came out of blabbering without knowing the context. If McManus had a question, he needed to ask it. Out of the corner of his eye, he saw the team's normally taciturn general manager, Hank Osbourne, try, and fail, to bite back a grin at the cat-and-mouse game playing out in front of him.

McManus heaved a frustrated sigh. "Let's start with why my sister felt the need to buy you for twenty-five thousand dollars!"

The force with which he asked the question practically rattled the wall of windows overlooking the practice field. Osbourn groaned. The team's community relations director jumped to her feet.

"To be fair, sir," she interjected. "Your sister did not buy Hudson per se. She paid twenty-five thousand dollars to go bowling with him."

McManus swung his computer monitor around angrily, revealing a photo of Noah and Charlotte, their lips locked in a deep kiss, outside of the penthouse the night before. "Does this look like bowling to you?!"

The woman sank back into her chair, not bothering to respond. Noah's left leg began to twitch before he rested his palm on his thigh to calm it.

"I've arranged to take some kids from the school bowling later this month," he told them. "The class that brings in the most cereal boxes to be donated to a local food bank will win the outing. On my dime."

The GM arched an eyebrow. "That's very magnanimous of you. Most guys would have washed their hands of the situation. And the team would have supported that decision."

Noah glanced over at the community relations director. "I'd like it if the team could provide the chaperones."

She nodded while Osbourn barked out a laugh.

"It's the least we can do," the GM said.

"If that's all." Noah moved to stand up.

Big mistake.

"No one is going anywhere," McManus snarled. "I want to know what possessed my sister to bid such an obscene amount."

"Have you asked her that, sir?" Noah was pushing his luck. He knew that. But he also knew he hadn't violated a single clause in his contract and that was the only hold this man had over him.

"I'm. Asking. You."

Noah kept his mouth shut and his gaze locked with his boss until McManus slammed his palms on his desk and vaulted from his seat.

"Do you realize I can trade you and you'd be emptying out your locker tomorrow? Or I could have your ass riding the bench for disciplinary reasons?"

Osbourn cleared his throat. "Technically, Jay—"

"Dammit, Hank, don't tell me what I can and can't do with my football team." McManus gestured wildly at Noah. "One of my players had his tongue shoved down my little sister's throat. Who the hell knows what else is going on between them?"

Despite the embarrassing situation, Noah had to feel for the guy. McManus' love for his sister was clear as day. Even if Charlotte was the man's kryptonite.

Noah didn't pity the guy enough to spill any tea, however. Besides, there wasn't anything else going on between them. He ignored the hollow feeling in his chest that came with that realization.

"With all due respect, sir. I don't kiss and tell."

McManus actually growled as he rounded his desk. The GM snapped to attention, putting an arm out to stop him mid-stride. Fortunately, reinforcements arrived at the same time.

"For crying out loud, Jay, cut it out," Charlotte demanded from the doorway.

She stormed into the room like an ancient crusader leading her troops into battle. Her long red hair billowed out behind her, the thud of her boot heels barely muted by the plush carpeting, and her eyes blue as flames. No one would mistake her for a mere princess the way she was carrying herself. She was a fucking queen, ready to slay dragons.

And he hated how turned on he was by the sight of her.

"Noah is right. You could have asked me! I would have told you. There's no need to bring out the torture devices," she admonished her brother.

Would she have? Would she have told her brother everything? He hoped not because he'd rather his boss not know how gullible Noah had been in falling for his sister's wiles. Mostly, though, he was embarrassed by the dick way he'd paid Charlotte back last night.

Time to hit the showers. McManus would have to make do with using his sister for a punching bag. He was pretty sure she wasn't averse to standing toe-to-toe with her domineering brother.

He was halfway out of his chair when a hand stalled him.

Noah locked eyes with Bridgett McManus, the owner's wife, who doubled as a ball-busting trial attorney. She was wearing her take-no-prisoners smile as she gestured for him to retake his seat.

"Hank, Meara, can we have the room please?" she asked, her tone indicating it wasn't a request.

The GM reluctantly released McManus, muttering something that only the two could hear, before gesturing for the community relations director to precede him out of the suite. McManus still had a death glare aimed at Noah. Mrs. McManus patted her husband's biceps, seeming to break the spell. Husband and wife exchanged a look that could have been an entire conversation. McManus blew out a sigh before nodding his head and dropping back into his chair.

His wife settled a hip on the corner of the desk and looked between Charlotte and Noah. "The media are churning out some wild stories about you two. It would help if we knew how to spin this. Who wants to go first?"

Oh, hell to the no.

Noah was on his feet and halfway to the door before anyone could stop him. Who knew his 4.93 forty-yard dash time would come in handy off the field?

"The media is well aware that I don't comment on my personal life. Tell them whatever you want, Charlotte. I need to get back to practice."

He was relieved when McManus didn't try to stop him. Halfway down the stairs, however, the staccato beat of boot heels on linoleum had his hackles back up.

"Noah, wait," Charlotte huffed.

Luckily, the practice facility was mostly deserted, this being the last free weekend before the season started. That didn't mean there weren't a few trainers and players milling around. The last thing Noah wanted was an audience for whatever zany thing Charlotte was going to say or do. She'd barely landed on the last step when he wrapped his fingers around her wrist and hustled her into the area behind the stairs.

"Hey," she protested.

Noah quickly released her. Mainly because touching her was torture. Also, he didn't believe in exerting his strength and size over women. She swept her hair back from her face and shot him a disgruntled look.

He was wrong. Her brother didn't have the same mouth. Charlotte's lips were much fuller and way more alluring. He knew from experience they were also pillowy soft. And as much as he wanted to trail his tongue over them right now, he was smart enough to know the danger in that move.

Stepping back, he crossed his arms over his chest. "If you're expecting a big thank you for bailing my ass out back there, you can forget it. I can take care of myself."

"What? No. I wasn't going to do that. Jay was being a beast for browbeating you." She pressed her fingers to her forehead. "I never intended for this to go this far."

"Mm. Should have thought about that before last night's grand gesture."

She jerked her head back. The wounded look in her eyes had his gut clenching. But it was the truth. She started it.

Should he have retaliated with their Internet breaking kiss? Probably not. Okay, definitely not. He was already paying for it, though, because now that he'd tasted her again, he was going to suffer the consequences every night for the foreseeable future.

Charlotte's sigh sounded resigned. "Look, I'm only in the States for a few more days. This should all blow over before the season starts. In the meantime, I'll make sure my brother stays off your back. I'll tell him something that will appease him."

"I'm sure you will."

Blue eyes narrowed. "What's that supposed to mean?"

"It means you have no problem spinning a story to fit your needs."

His eyes were drawn to her long neck as he watched her swallow whatever biting retort she intended. The gold chain she wore winked at him, drawing his gaze lower. She dragged in a deep breath, giving him a bird's-eye view of her breasts rising and falling beneath the form-fitting T-shirt with her company's logo emblazoned across the front.

Noah dragged his eyes just in time to see the corners of her mouth turn up to form a sly smile. He had the sudden thought that he should protect the family jewels. She took a step closer. He forced himself not to react to her nearness, but the effort was moot. Every nerve in his body jumped to attention, dammit.

"Well, it wouldn't be—" Her fingers brushed against his chest when she lifted her hands to make air quotes. "—spinning my story to say that you kissed me against my will. Twice."

He chuckled at her bravado. "The photo evidence says otherwise. Your hands were all over my ass."

Score one for the home team.

Her lips quivered until she sank her teeth into the bottom one. He needed to get away before he did something stupid. Like kiss her again. He took a giant step back and turned in the direction of the locker room.

"But duly noted," he called over his shoulder. "Next time, Princess, if you want me to kiss you, you're going to need to beg for it."

CHARLOTTE SIGHED as she pushed the folder across the conference table.

"Don't sound so glum. You don't have to make a decision right away," Bridgett said as she refilled her water bottle from the pitcher at the coffee bar in the back of the room. "It's important that you take your time. Find someone with a similar vision to yours."

"But we've interviewed twelve qualified candidates this week and I don't feel right giving any of them control of my company."

Bridgett chuckled as she sat back down. "Now you know how I felt interviewing nannies." She sobered up and reached across the table to grab Charlotte's hand. "You aren't giving your baby up. You're just putting her in the hands of someone with a bit more experience managing a company that's had a meteoric rise. And you'll always have me looking over the shoulder of whomever you choose."

"Yeah, but I can't keep asking you to fly back and forth between here and London." Charlotte shook her head. "You put practicing law on hold for a while to be a more hands-on parent. And these past three years, it seems like you've worked harder than ever."

She didn't mention the fact that she suspected Bridgett was staying on out of guilt. As some sort of compensation for Charlotte carrying her children. The idea that her sister-in-law might be feeling obligated to help at Truly didn't sit well.

Bridgett waved her hand around the conference room. "And during that time, my kids were right upstairs. Your brother built-out these offices so we could both work from home. In fact—" Her lips curved up in a mischievous grin. "There is plenty of office space here. You could always move your headquarters back to the States. We'd love having you around more."

Charlotte would love that, too. But watching Jay and Bridgett with their beautiful children—the Christmas card worthy family she helped create—was just too painful. Not when she wanted that for herself.

Her brother and her sister-in-law would be crushed if they knew she thought that way. They were always enthusiastic about including her. But she didn't want to be the fifth wheel for the rest of her life. Besides, deep down, she believed Jay and Bridgett did it to thank her. And their kindness felt a lot like pity sometimes.

"And give up my friends and fans in London?" she quipped. "I couldn't." No need for her sister-in-law to know that Charlotte's friends didn't understand her need to do something with her life besides living off her father's fortune.

"We'll work something out, then." Bridgett withdrew her hand.

Charlotte didn't have time to contemplate the flat tone of her sister-in-law's voice because Gray and Vivi were bounding into the room, Jay on their heels.

"Mom, we stopped and got cookies on the way home," Gray announced as he crawled into his mother's lap. "I got you a peanut butter cookie."

"I got you a lemon one, Aunt Charlie." Vivi scrambled into Charlotte's lap, nearly dropping the bag containing the cookie.

"Cookies?" Bridgett arched an eyebrow at her husband.

Jay dropped two backpacks into an empty chair. "It was a special occasion. They finished their first week of school."

Grayson shrieked with laughter when Jay tilted Bridgett's chair back so he could kiss her. Charlotte looked down at her niece, who was ignoring her parents' display, instead dissecting her chocolate chip cookie, and putting it into her mouth, piece-by-piece.

"This doesn't look like your school uniform." She tugged at the Blaze jersey Vivian wore with her uniform skort and white sneakers.

"Friday is Spirit Day," Grayson explained as he snuck a taste of his mother's cookie. "Everyone wears jerseys for their favorite team."

"Ah," Charlotte said. "I'll bet there were a lot of Blaze jerseys."

Vivian huffed out a frustrated sounding breath. "All the girls wore Noah's jersey." Her bottom lip curled. "Even the teachers."

"Yeah, our teacher said she didn't even like football, but Noah is now her favorite player," Grayson added. "She even got Noah's jersey for her nieces, and they live in Florida."

Charlotte exchanged a puzzled look with Bridgett.

"What did Noah do to become so popular?" she asked.

"It's 'coz you've got lots of fans. And he kissed you," Grayson said. "Mrs. Ruttle told the class you're going to get married."

Her brother muttered something that sounded savage.

"What?!" In her shock, Charlotte almost dumped her niece onto the floor. Her stomach was already there. "Who started that rumor?"

Jay's long-time assistant, Lincoln Harris, strolled into the conference room carrying a stack of folders. "It's everywhere," he said. "And we can't keep Noah's jersey in stock. Neither can the league." He grinned at Charlotte. "Your Trulies have all become instant Blaze fans." He gave his boss a thumbs up. "The network has made Sunday's game its game of the week. Everyone is interested in the Blaze QB now that Charlie is his main squeeze."

This time her brother groaned.

"Hey, man, more eyes on your team means more money in your pocket." Linc shrugged. "I say let the fauxmance play out. While they are all speculating when the wedding will be, they'll be scooping up jerseys and boosting our television ratings."

Vivian grew stiff in Charlotte's arms. "You promised you wouldn't marry him," she whimpered.

"No one is marrying Noah Hudson. Least of all me." Charlotte gently transferred her niece to one of the other chairs before standing. She aimed a death glare at Linc, her friend and confidant for nearly a decade. "Shame on you for helping to perpetuate this nonsense."

Linc's eyes went round against his caramel skin. "Ah, come on, Charlie. You've known me long enough to recognize my sarcasm when you hear it. I don't like these stupid rumors any more than you do." He put his hands on his hips. "But you're a successful businesswoman now. Everyone is going to come for you. You've got to roll with it and figure out a way to make it work for you and your brand."

Great.

Now even Linc was pointing out her flaws as a CEO. And the worst part? He was right. She wasn't cut out to run a company.

She snatched up her bag and draped the strap over her shoulder. "I'm going to catch a barre class."

"Aren't you coming with us to the back-to-school picnic?" Grayson asked.

"Oh, no." Charlotte shook her head. "I think it would be best if I stayed away from Shepard Academy for a while."

"Charlie, wait." Bridgett handed her son off to Jay. "I have an idea about the CEO search I want to float by you."

That was the last thing Charlotte wanted to think about

right now. She waved her sister-in-law off. "My brain is a little fried right now. Let's talk about it tomorrow."

She was acting rude. Especially after everything Bridgett did to help with Truly You. Charlotte hadn't evolved as much as she'd thought, obviously. She hurried out of the conference room before she did or said something else that might reveal how childish and insecure she still was.

SIX

THE HAPPY HOUR crowd at Devlin's had thinned out by eight-thirty that evening. Noah sat on his usual stool at the dark end of the bar, closest to the kitchen. The regulars were used to seeing him parked there on Friday nights before a home game. After all, he'd been sitting in that same spot every football season for the past seven years.

It was tradition for the starting quarterback to take the offensive line out for a pricey steak dinner before the season opener. For years, that dinner happened at the bougie steakhouse owned by the Blaze MVP quarterback, Shane Devlin. It wasn't customary to include the backup QB, but Devlin wasn't one for rules and protocol. He'd always insisted Noah join them.

"To soak up whatever knowledge you can," he'd explained.

Those preseason dinners evolved into regular Friday night dinners between the two quarterbacks during the season, the veteran baller quizzing Noah on every play in the playbook just in case he'd have to come into the game for Devlin.

"I don't want you blowing a lead if I get sidelined," he'd grumble.

When Devlin finally hung up his cleats, everyone on the offense just assumed they'd continue going to his restaurant for the annual dinner. So did the former QB. He lorded over the meal like the elder statesman he was, before drilling Noah one-on-one on the game plan after everyone left.

Noah's father believed his son would have an easier time with fans and the media had Devlin left Baltimore and not cast such a long shadow over his replacement's career. There were days when Noah agreed. Other days, however, he was grateful for the wizened quarterback's guidance.

Today was not one of those days.

"After months of trying to keep your image afloat, you have to go and do something that gets you to the top of every damn search engine in the world. Why would you be such a dumbass as to get caught kissing the owner's sister?" Devlin hung a dishtowel onto his shoulder before leveling a "give-it-to-me" stare at Noah.

The questions had been flying all week. From his teammates, the media, even his family. For the most part, Noah had no trouble redirecting everyone back to the topic of football and the upcoming game. If he were being honest, he was glad to have everyone's attention on something other than last year's disastrous season. Come Sunday, he would prove himself on the field and everyone would forget about the past. And his infamous kiss with Charlotte Davis would be dubbed old news.

"Unless you have some game strategy to impart, I'm out of here." Noah guzzled what remained of his beer.

Devlin shook his head. "Damn, man, you are like a crypt about your private life." He sighed. "My only game pointers are to test their right corner early on. I've been watching his preseason film, and Bailey doesn't look fully recovered from his knee injury last year."

Noah thought the same thing. "Of course, Bailey could be playing all of us."

"That's why you better be sure to test him with a ball he can't pick." Devlin turned toward a commotion at the other end of the bar. "Speak of the devil."

"Bailey's here?"

Devlin was suddenly wearing a shit-eating grin. "Even better. Your girlfriend is here."

The maître D was leading Charlotte right to Noah, giving him no chance to escape.

"I told you Mr. Devlin was still here," the maître D said. "And someone else you will be glad to see." The guy winked at Charlotte.

Noah wouldn't exactly describe her expression as glad. Irked would be more like it. He was pretty sure she hadn't expected to find him there. She recovered well, though, a dazzling smile forming on her lips.

"Shane," she gushed. "It's so good to see you. And I couldn't leave town without enjoying one of your fabulous Niçoise salads."

Devlin came out from behind the bar and wrapped his arms around her. "I would have been insulted if you had."

The smile she gave the ex-quarterback was genuine. "How are Carly and the kids?"

"Powering through the first week of school," Devlin replied.

"And Troy?" she asked. "It must be hard sending your little brother off to college."

Devlin laughed. "You must not spend much time around know-it-all teenagers." His face softened. "Don't you dare repeat this, but I miss having him around. He's settling in nicely, though. And he's barely two hours away. In fact, I'm heading there with a care package tomorrow."

Noah long suspected his mentor was a big softy when it came to his younger brother. Troy had been a fixture in the locker room since Noah's first season with the Blaze. Despite the former quarterback's bluster, everyone knew how much he adored the kid.

Devlin narrowed his eyes at Noah, then gestured at a vacant stool that was too close for comfort. "Hudson has been saving you a seat. I'll get your salad ordered. You want a glass of Prosecco with that?"

Charlotte didn't move. Neither did Noah. Devlin appeared to be frozen, too, his gaze shifting back and forth between them like he was watching some invisible tennis match.

A gentleman stands when a lady enters the room, his mother's voice admonished his conscience.

Noah got to his feet. "Actually, I was just leaving."

"Interesting," Devlin murmured.

Charlotte ducked her chin and slid onto the barstool next to the one Noah had just vacated. "There are a few paps outside. You might want to go out the back."

Christ.

Devlin cleared his throat. "Too late. There are already a few cellphones aimed this way. I'll make the rounds and ask them to put them away." He clapped Noah on the shoulder. "But it might be a smart play to stay and give the people what they want for a few."

Seriously? Hadn't the dickhead just been riding his ass about getting involved with Charlotte?

Noah's frustration must have shown in his expression, because a rare smile settled on Devlin's lips.

"I'm going to have to revoke your man card if you leave this beautiful woman to eat her dinner alone."

Shooting his mentor a WTF grin, Noah sat back down. He waved the bartender over. "Prosecco for the lady and sparkling water with lime for me."

"I didn't know you were here," she murmured to the bar top.

"Yeah, your face said it all."

She whirled her chin around to glare at him. Her mouth opened and closed a few times before she faced forward again. The bartender placed their drinks in front of them. Charlotte snatched hers up, clinking it against Noah's glass.

"Here's to the end of a shitty week," she said before taking a gulp.

"I'll drink to that." Noah took a sip. "Although my week has been pretty stellar."

"You enjoy dodging cameras and ignoring insinuating headlines?"

He shrugged. "Comes with the job. Although Bucky Kincaid has been abnormally quiet, so I'll take that as a win."

She pondered the inside of her glass. "He has, hasn't he? Well, at least one good thing has come out of this situation." She cocked her head to the side and shot him a smarmy grin. "You're welcome."

"Why is it that you're always demanding I thank you? Especially since you're the reason we're in this mess."

"Excuse me? You were the one doing the kissing." Her gaze dropped to his mouth, lingering there for longer than necessary.

His junk was suddenly painful against the zipper of his pants.

"You didn't seem to mind," he drawled, mentally slapping himself for staying with the provocative subject.

Her eyes shot back to clash with his just as Devlin returned with her salad.

"Thank you," she said to their host.

Devlin leaned across the bar and kissed her on the cheek. "On the house. But next time you're in town, don't wait until the last minute to stop by. I'm headed home." He looked between them both. "You two behave now. Charlie, I'll let your security team know you'll be exiting through the kitchen when you're finished."

"Give my love to Carly," she called after him.

An uncomfortable silence settled over them. Charlotte pushed her salad around on her plate. Noah looked around the bar. Everyone was still sneaking glances at them.

"Will you hurry up and eat that," he said gruffly. "We're going to have to leave here together, and I haven't got all night."

This time, when she turned to glare at him, Noah really looked at her. Taking in the dark circles beneath her eyes and the pinched line of her lips, he instantly felt like a douche. A strand of her hair had escaped her ponytail and was stuck to the side of her face. Instinctively, he reached for it, gently settling the silky strands behind her ear. He wasn't sure, but he thought Charlotte might have stopped breathing. He was sure he'd heard one of the waitresses sigh, though.

"Tell me about your sucky week," he asked quietly.

She blinked a few times before absently licking her lower lip. Noah bit back a groan. He snagged one of her olives and popped it in his mouth to keep from touching her again.

"I've been interviewing potential CEOs for my company," she announced with a heavy sigh before spearing some lettuce with her fork.

Her words surprised him. In London, she'd been so animated about Truly You. She was about to take it global.

And he could easily see how thrilled and proud she was about the prospect. Had she gotten bored playing businesswoman?

"You don't want to run it anymore?" He hated how he instantly thought the worst of her. Except her track record spoke for itself.

"The last thing I want to do is hand it over to someone else," she replied sharply.

He deserved her pique for being so judgmental. "Then why do it?"

Her gaze remained focused on her salad. "Because I'm not good at running it."

Something snapped inside his chest at the sorrowful way she uttered the words. "Bullshit."

She whipped her chin up to meet his gaze.

Noah stopped fighting his body and lifted his palm to her face. "Look what you've done with it so far? Christ, little girls are buying my jersey because they adore you and the company you created. You did that."

Charlotte leaned into his palm. Her eyes were shiny. "Maybe. But there's so much more to it than simply creating a product. I don't have the skill-set necessary to keep it all afloat."

There was dejection in those beautiful blue eyes of hers and Noah suddenly wanted to punch someone.

Or kiss her until she forgot all about her troubles.

He dropped his hand from her cheek and nicked a cherry tomato from her plate instead.

"So, you hire someone with those skills. A CEO willing to teach them to you."

She smiled and the hardness in Noah's chest relaxed.

"You sound like Bridgett."

"I'll take that as a compliment." He popped the tomato in his mouth. "She's pretty badass."

Charlotte ate her salad with a bit more gusto after that.

"I know I'm being too picky," she said when she slid her empty plate forward. "It's hard, though. I keep thinking I've failed by handing Truly over to someone else." She laughed softly. "You're the only person I've admitted that to."

A warm feeling replaced the tightness in his chest. "My Meemaw always says everything looks better when you put your fears out into the world."

"Meemaw?"

"My grandmother." He knew how lucky he was to have a grandparent still in his life. His father's mother, Meemaw, had been as involved in his upbringing as his parents.

"Huh. I didn't know my grandparents. My dad's parents were long gone before I was born. And my mom was the black sheep of her family. I only met her father right before he died. Tell me, what's this Meemaw of yours like?" she asked wistfully.

She's a lot like you, he wanted to say. Able to hold her own in a world that constantly wanted to knock her down. Creative and street smart.

"You'd like her. You're both tall," he said instead.

Charlotte laughed. It was a lovely sound. He had the sudden vision of her laughing in bed, her hair a riotous mess against the pillows, and her body flushed with passion. Shifting in his seat, he remembered their audience, their attention all discreetly focused on the two of them.

"She sounds lovely," Charlotte said.

"Mmm. Except she thinks this—" He gestured between them. "—is real, and she is insisting I bring you to her eighty-fifth birthday party."

Her joy evaporated. "Oh."

Noah was suddenly angry at himself for thinking any part of this was real. For thinking she'd jump at the chance to show up on his arm at a dear old lady's birthday party. They were worlds apart. He needed to remember that.

He got to his feet. "I need to study some film tonight."

"Oh," she repeated. "Of course." She began to rummage through her purse, presumably for a tip.

"I got this." He left a fifty on the bar and reached for her elbow.

She shot him a haughty look.

"Cameras," he whispered through his gritted teeth.

That got her attention and had her hustling into the kitchen.

"This way," she said as they wound their way through the prep area and back to the cold storage.

Noah had to wonder how many times she'd escaped through restaurant kitchens and hotel bars. They turned down a narrow hallway. A red exit sign blinked above a steel door. He put his hand on her back to propel her forward.

Of course, she stopped.

Before he could even react, her arms were looped around his neck and her body was pressed against his.

"Thank you for listening back there," she said right before her lips crashed into his.

She tasted like lemon and sparkling wine. His hands were on her hips, pulling her closer without him even realizing it. She dug her fingers into his skull, angling his mouth to give her better access, and he was here for it. For all of it.

For all of her.

He leaned his back against the wall and let her have her way with his mouth. In the meantime, his hands explored the curves of her body ruthlessly. When he palmed one of her breasts, a keening sound rose from deep in her throat. His own chest rumbled at her responsiveness.

Christ, she was perfect.

Charlotte kissed him with such reckless abandon it turned him on as much as it scared the shit out of him. He wanted her with a fervor like he'd never wanted anything else. His desire was all-consuming, almost making him forget where they were and how vulnerable they were to having their every move documented.

A pot clanging in the kitchen behind him brought him back to his senses. He gently threaded his fingers through her hair and tugged her mouth from his. Her lips were swollen and wet. Letting out a groan, he traced his tongue over them before shifting her body away from his. He couldn't think while they fitted together like that.

She adjusted the collar of his shirt. "There. Now you can't accuse me of never thanking you."

Noah smacked his head softly against the wall. It looked like it was taking her effort to stop her hands from touching him, but she finally managed it. Her smile was wily as she backed toward the exit door.

"And, for the record, I had every intention of thanking you in London," she was saying.

He crossed his arms over his chest. "Hard to do when you ghosted me."

"Only temporarily. I didn't want you to get caught with me in your room."

His breath hitched. He hadn't even considered that.

"I came back later," she continued. "With scones."

The roaring was back in his ears, but this time it had nothing to do with passion.

"I overheard you talking to your teammates."

Oh, no. No, no, no.

He wracked his brain, trying to recall exactly what he'd

said. It wouldn't paint him in a good light, that was for sure. But he'd been angry. He'd felt betrayed by her disappearance. Christ. He was an idiot.

"You heard that?" he pushed out through the Sahara Desert that was his mouth.

Her chin wobbled a bit, then she nodded. This conversation was costing her, but still she soldiered on.

"Charlotte—" he choked out.

She held up a hand. "No worries. I get that I'm not everyone's cup of tea. And with you, I'm 'not even close.'"

Had her words been fists, they would have hit him squarely in the jaw.

"Goodbye, Noah. Have a great season. You deserve it."

With that, she slipped out the exit door. It took Noah a moment to pick up his balls from the floor and stagger after her. One of her bodyguards was already closing the door to a black SUV by the time he made it outside.

Let her go, he heard his father's voice say to his subconscious. *You need to focus on Sunday's game.*

He was still breathing hard when the SUV drove away. No wonder she'd looked straight through him all these years. All because his ego had taken a blow when he woke up to find her gone. He kicked at the ground, scattering pebbles into the air.

His father was right, though. Noah couldn't afford the distraction of a sexy mouth and come-hither blue eyes, no matter how much guilt he was carrying. Not when his career was on the line. If he continued to be a pariah in the media or stink up the playing field, his days were numbered with the Blaze. And very likely all of football.

And, as much as his body wanted to argue differently, Charlotte Davis was too complicated, too sophisticated, too much of a whirling dervish to fit into the quiet life he needed to concentrate on staying in the game. Now all he needed was a long, cold shower to convince his body of that fact. He stormed toward the valet stand at the front of the restaurant, grateful when he saw the paps had dispersed for the evening.

SEVEN

"WE ARE ON TV AGAIN!" Grayson waved at the crowd as he jumped up and down.

Sure enough, the television monitor inside the owner's suite at the Blaze stadium displayed a shot of the skybox and its occupants for the fourth time in the first half. Every time Noah completed a pass, or in this case, a touchdown, the cameras panned this way. The crowd roared its approval when the Blaze kicker sent the ball through the uprights for the extra point.

Charlotte clapped enthusiastically along with them. She was happy to see the Blaze—and Noah—playing so well. She was not happy that the network kept zooming in on her.

She slumped back down into her seat beside Sophie Osbourne. The young woman had the audacity to laugh.

"It's not funny," Charlotte ground out through the smile she kept plastered on her face just in case the cameras panned back to them.

"Oh, come on." Sophie elbowed her. "At least the media isn't crucifying him anymore."

Charlotte gestured to the field. "Because he's playing brilliantly. I have nothing to do with it. I swear, the media sensationalizes everything. It's obnoxious."

"Well, maybe you two should stop giving them sexy videos to use as click-bait."

Sophie swiped through her phone, sighing when she pulled up the video someone in the bar shot the other night. It featured Noah tucking her hair behind her ear. The stupid clip was all over social media. Charlotte hated having the private moment invaded, much less micro-analyzed by sports reports and the average Joe.

"That is an incredibly romantic gesture for two people who are just friends." Sophie said the last two words in a sing-song voice.

It was romantic.

She hadn't expected to find Noah at Devlin's Friday evening. All she wanted was a salad, a quiet place to think. Instead, she got a side dish of delicious jock to go with her meal while his mesmerizing touch scattered her brain cells.

It was getting hard to pretend she didn't like the guy when he kept touching her and seducing her to bare her soul. Why was it that she was comfortable telling him things she couldn't tell anyone else? And then, as if that wasn't enough, she kissed him. Ignoring his dumb challenge that she had to beg him for a kiss, she took his mouth like she had a right to it.

Her cheeks grew warm just thinking about it. Thank God nobody in the kitchen had their cell phones armed and ready. They would have gotten a screen full. For heaven's sake, she was practically dry humping the man in the hallway.

A day and a half later, she still couldn't fathom what had possessed her to jump him. Maybe it was that she knew she might never have the opportunity to savor his kiss again. And she wanted to thank him. He'd accused her of not being gracious. Simply saying the words would have probably been more appropriate than mauling the man, she realized too late.

Except Noah didn't exactly object. In fact, he'd kissed her back as though she was his type. As if he wanted to kiss her.

Don't read too much into it. He's a guy, she kept reminding herself.

The expression on his face when she revealed what she'd overheard three years ago puzzled her, however. He actually looked pained to have his words thrown back at him. More likely, he was simply embarrassed to be caught berating the team owner's sister and the look she saw was nothing but guilt.

She was just being whimsical, hoping it was something else.

"It is nice to see Noah getting positive press, though," Sophie mused. "He's a decent guy who deserves to be treated that way."

"If you like him so much, why don't you date him?"

The words came out of Charlotte's mouth with a bit more bite than they should have. Which was ridiculous because Sophie was perfect for Noah. Sweet, creative, and, having grown up around football, she wasn't easily intimidated by the jock persona.

They would look cute together, too. Sophie wouldn't have to worry about giving up her heels so she wouldn't tower over Noah. The young artist had outgrown her pink hair—it was now strawberry blonde—and ditched the nose ring she'd taunted her father with as a teen. They'd have adorable babies

That was *not* jealousy knotting up Charlotte's stomach.

"No thank you," Sophie replied. "Athletes are not my thing. Especially football players."

A melancholy look settled on the younger woman's face.

"I'm getting the sense there is a story here." Charlotte shifted in her chair so that she was facing her friend.

Sophie's laugh lacked any humor. "Just me being naïve in high school. Never again."

"What happened?"

"It's a tale as old as time," Sophie said with a wave of her hand. "I got a little too star-struck when the quarterback of the football team claimed to like me. I was a geeky sophomore with outrageous outfits and wild hair. What could the prom king possibly see in me? But it was nice to finally sit at the cool kids' table for once, you know?"

Charlotte didn't know. Her trust fund put her front and center at the cool kids' table every day of her life. A twinge of guilt nibbled at her. Would she even have paid attention to someone like Sophie?

"Anyway, it turns out he was using me for an intro to my dad. He was trying to get a walk on spot with a D one football program and he thought a nudge from the Blaze GM would help." She shook her head. "Luckily, my dad saw right through him."

Charlotte squeezed her friend's hand. "You're very fortunate to have your dad looking out for you."

This time, Sophie's laugh was genuine. "I didn't think so at the time." She quickly sobered up, a soft smile forming on her lips as she peered over at her father and his second wife, Annabeth, the mother of former Blaze star, Will Connelly. "But he turned out to be pretty cool."

Asia Dupree-Carter, media director for the team, dropped into a chair on Charlotte's other side. "Can I bend your ear for a minute?"

"Sure," Charlotte replied. "What's up?"

"I've been fielding requests all day for a statement."

Charlotte waited for Asia to elaborate. "A statement?" she asked when it was clear Asia wasn't going to elaborate.

"About you and Noah."

"Uh, oh." Sophie sounded more smug than concerned.

"Does the team normally comment on the players' personal lives?" Charlotte demanded.

"It depends on the situation. And this situation sits firmly under the no comment heading." She leaned forward in her chair. "But now I'm in a pickle. We've been working behind the scenes to subtly elevate Noah's image among the fans."

Charlotte snorted a laugh. "Yeah, I saw how well that went last weekend."

Asia groaned. "That's on me. I didn't see it coming." She fanned herself with the program she was holding. "But honestly, can you blame them? And from where I sit, you looked like you were enjoying your purchase."

"It wasn't a purchase. It was a rescue," Charlotte snapped.

"Whatever you say," Asia said with a chuckle. "But your 'rescue' is why I'm in a pickle." She sighed. "We invited a young heart transplant patient from Make-A-Wish to the game. He's going to meet with Noah after."

"That's sweet, but I'm not seeing the pickle."

"His sister, who, according to her mom, couldn't care less about football, came today because she wants to meet you."

"Me?"

Asia nodded. "Charlotte, there are little girls in the stadium wearing your affirmation bracelets, Noah's jersey, and waving signs cheering him on. The media is eating it up. No one else in the league is getting this kind of adoration. For Noah's sake, we need to tap into it."

Charlotte fingered the three silver bracelets circling her wrist.

"What are you proposing?" Sophie asked.

"That Charlotte join Noah at the meet and greet with the family after the game."

"With cameras rolling?" Charlotte choked out.

"Nope." Asia shook her head. "That would take all the attention away from Dalton, the little boy. We do want media exposure, obviously, so we've arranged a little press conference for Dalton and his family afterward."

"Oh, I like that," Sophie cooed. "They can tell everyone how nice Noah is. And Charlie, too."

Asia nodded. "Obviously there will be cameras as you both exit the stadium. But you two can just walk out with no comment. Like friends would do. Nothing scandalous."

"Good, because we are just friends." Technically, Charlotte wasn't sure what she was to Noah. Friends would be nice, though. She ignored Sophie's inelegant snort.

"'Just friends' works for me," Asia said.

"What did Noah say?" Charlotte wasn't committing to anything without running it by him first.

Asia rolled her eyes. "You know how he is. Tight-lipped about his personal life. Except it's a little hard for you both to keep your friendship under wraps any longer. He said he'd do whatever you wanted."

"Aww." Sophie slapped Charlotte on the shoulder. "That's sweet."

It was Charlotte's turn to roll her eyes. "What does my brother think?" she asked Asia.

All three of them turned to focus their attention on Jay, who was playing a video game with Grayson while the game on the field was at halftime.

"I don't consult him with these types of things. I leave that up to the GM."

"So, this is Hank's idea?"

Asia nodded solemnly. "Hank felt every shot the media fired at Noah last season like it was directed at him.

"I'll say," Sophie chimed in. "Deep down, my dad is a big softy when it comes to his players."

Charlotte sucked in a deep breath. She'd felt those shots, too. Every one of them. Especially the ones Bucky Kincaid used to smear Noah's reputation. Because she was the guilty party who brought Noah into Bucky's crosshairs.

"Okay." She agreed before she could change her mind.

NOAH HAD JUST PLAYED the game of his life. Thirty-one completed passes—three of them for touchdowns—without a single interception. He'd even scrambled for the first down twice. But what did the media want to focus on? Charlotte Davis. More specifically, why he couldn't keep his hands off her. As if he knew the answer to that. It had taken every ounce of composure he had to stand at the podium and deflect their ridiculous questions about his personal life.

"You handled that well," Asia said as they exited the elevator, taking them to the stadium's private suites. "I know it wasn't easy."

He didn't bother to answer, afraid that he might take out his frustrations on the woman who'd had his back the previous season. Especially when the media were piling on.

"Thank you for doing this today," she continued, her trendy sneakers squeaking on the concrete floor.

"I'll do anything for the kids. Especially the sick ones." He shifted one of the game balls from one hand to the other. Most guys would hold on to a keepsake from a monumental game. But Noah knew the ball would do more good to a kid recovering from a heart transplant than it would sitting in a dusty display case.

"Charlotte is already inside." She handed him a surgical mask. "Dalton is vulnerable to germs. He's also a bit worn out from all the excitement of the day. His mom asks that we keep this brief."

"I should have skipped the presser," he murmured as he secured the mask over his mouth.

Asia laughed. "If only."

Noah was prepared for a subdued mood to greet him when he entered the suite. The little boy still wasn't out of the woods. He should have known that wouldn't be the case with Charlotte there. Despite her leather pants and willowy peasant blouse, she was on the floor with Dalton on her lap. The two were playing a game on her phone. Beside her, a girl who appeared to be about middle school age sat hanging on every word Charlotte said, a worshipful look in her eyes.

"Here he is," Charlotte exclaimed. "The man destined to be named the player of the week." Her eyes were smiling as she led the room in applause.

Dalton gingerly rose from her lap and extended his fist for a bump. "I knew you could do it," the little boy said. "You're going to be the MVP for sure this year."

Noah's throat grew tight. It was humbling to have this kid believing in him with such blind faith. This is what it is all about, he thought. This right here.

He crouched down on his haunches. "Well, that would be cool, wouldn't it? I'll do my best. But you have to promise to do what the doctors and your parents say so you can come to the ceremony with me."

Dalton's brown eyes went wide. "Really?"

"Really." Noah bumped the kid's fist again. "And to seal

the deal, I brought you a game ball. How do you want it signed?"

They spent ten more minutes with Dalton and his family before Asia herded them toward the elevator.

"It's time for your press conference, little man," she said.

Dalton looked up at Noah with pure delight in his eyes. "I'm going to be on TV," he said.

"Try not to get nervous up there," Noah advised. "Just pretend they're all in their underwear."

The little boy belly laughed. His parents thanked both Noah and Charlotte for meeting with their kids.

Charlotte tousled Dalton's hair. "Next time I'm in town, I need some Minecraft tips. You play better than anyone I know."

The doors to the elevator headed to the players' exit opened first. Asia inclined her head in that direction.

"That's your ride," she said to Noah. "Remember, just smile and walk."

Noah followed Charlotte into the elevator, where both shed their masks as soon as the doors closed. Charlotte gulped in a breath. Then another before bending over at the waist.

"Hey, are you okay?" He laid a hand against her back.

She trembled beneath his palm. Then he heard the sobs. He punched the stop button, causing the elevator to lurch to a halt. No way was he going to let the media see her like this.

"Shh." He gathered her up in his arms. "It's okay."

"It's not," she cried. "He's just a little boy. It's not fair."

It wasn't fair. But then Noah already knew life wasn't fair. He tucked his hand beneath her long hair and skimmed his palm along her back. Her eyes were shining when she looked up at him.

"It just as easily could be Grayson or Vivian needing a transplant," she said between gasps.

Her devotion to her niece and nephew was endearing. Noah pulled her into his arms. "But it's not either of them. And even if it were, they'd survive."

She curled into his chest. "But those parents. It has to be agonizing for them. I don't know how they are getting through it."

Memories came hurtling back. "It's no picnic for anyone when a family is going through something like that."

Charlotte went still. A long minute later, she shifted against him, lifting her chin so her eyes met his. "Why does it sound like you're speaking from experience?"

He wiped at the moisture beneath her eyes with his thumbs before speaking. "My sister had leukemia. They discovered it when she was twelve. It was the nasty kind. It took five years before they cured her of it."

Her hands traveled up along his chest, where she settled her palms. "Oh, Noah. That must have been devastating for your family. How old were you?"

"I was five when she first got sick." He swallowed painfully.

"It must have been difficult for you to understand."

He nodded. "I just wanted everything to go back to the way it was. My parents were stressed all the time. About Alexandra and money and..." He shrugged. "I did my best to be helpful and invisible at the same time."

She drew in a deep breath. "Oh."

"Don't. It all worked out. Alex is fine. Thriving, actually. Married with two kids. We all got through it. Dalton and his family will, too."

Charlotte's cellphone buzzed in her pocket. She tugged it out and glanced at the screen. "My security team is about to call S.W.A.T. to get us out of this elevator." She gave him a wane smile.

"Time to face the music." He reached for the start button.

"Wait!" She dabbed at her eyes. "I must look a mess."

He shook his head. "You always look beautiful."

A smile lit up her face. He felt a fission of pride at giving her a reason to smile. Even though what he'd told her was true. She was beautiful.

He punched the button to get the elevator moving again. A member of her security team was waiting when the doors opened. Behind him was a horde of cameras pointed in their direction. Reporters shouted questions as they walked the gauntlet of media outlets lined up in the long hallway.

"You were great today, Hudson," one of the janitors yelled out.

Charlotte linked her arm through Noah's and beamed at him. "You were better than great today," she murmured. "You were amazing."

Something in his chest swelled at her praise. Cameras whirred as he waved at the janitorial crew. Everyone was yelling at them to look this way or that, but Charlotte kept her eyes focused on him, a wily smile on her face. He laughed at her cheekiness.

Having navigated the maze of media, her security team steered them toward the doors leading to the private parking lot. The area was blessedly empty.

"Give us a minute," Noah said to her bodyguards.

Charlotte nodded when both men looked at her for confirmation.

"We need to hustle if you're going to make that flight," one of them said, before disappearing through the door.

"Are you going to be okay?" Noah asked once they were alone.

She nodded. "You have a way of making things better."

She reached up and adjusted the collar of his shirt. "Thank you."

He stepped in closer, instead of doing what he should—take a giant step back. Way back. With a soft sigh, she leaned in, closing the remaining space between their bodies.

"I like your other thank you technique," he murmured against the corner of her lips.

"You said you wouldn't initiate a kiss again unless I begged," she whispered.

"I lied."

Noah had asked for these few minutes to reassure himself she was alright. But now all he could think about was kissing her. The little hum of pleasure she made when his mouth settled over hers detonated something inside him. He tangled his fingers in her hair, angling her mouth so he could take what he wanted like a marauding pirate.

Teeth and tongues collided as Charlotte did her own plundering while anxious sighs of need escaped the back of her throat. No other woman responded to Noah's kisses quite like she did. Her hunger was just as intense as his.

And if he had a lick of sense left in his brain, he would be running for the hills. Because this wasn't any ordinary woman in his arms. This was Charlotte Davis. Princess Charlotte. Wealthy. Privileged. World famous. And so out of his league it was ridiculous.

A loud banging sounded on the exit door. Charlotte tore her mouth away. Noah released her immediately. They both were breathing hard. She pressed her fingers to her lips. He dragged his through his hair to keep from reaching for her again.

"My flight back to London leaves in two hours," she whispered.

He nodded, afraid if he spoke that he'd embarrass himself

by begging her to stay. Which was absurd, because she'd never choose Noah. Hell, she probably had another guy, a sophisticated playboy, waiting in Europe for her. The two would be laughing at her lapse in judgment over a bottle of ridiculously priced champagne later tonight.

She adjusted her blouse and her hair, but when her eyes met his, they were bewildered, as if she was confused about what to do. Noah knew what had to be done, though.

"Let's get you out of here," he said, despite it being the last thing he wanted. "You need to get back to ruling your cosmetics empire. You've got a CEO to hire, remember?"

He'd somehow muffed the play because her eyes were back to being glassy.

"I was trying not to think about that," she said.

Christ. Now he'd upset her again.

"You'll figure it out. You're a smart woman. Trust your instincts."

She gasped in a breath, then her lips formed a shaky grin. "You think I'm smart?"

The banging on the door grew more urgent.

"Not if you miss your flight," he teased, trying to lighten things up.

He pushed the door open. The confusion was back in her eyes. Her bodyguards rushed her into the SUV. She gave Noah an aggravated wave just before one of her team closed the back passenger door. Noah responded with a nod. He turned to the bodyguard.

"Take good care of her," he ground out through his tight jaw.

"Always. It's in the job description." The guy jumped into the passenger seat and the SUV sped off.

<h1 style="text-align:center">EIGHT</h1>

CHARLOTTE GROANED and dropped her head into her hands. "My lenders are getting twitchy."

When the image on the computer screen remained silent, she forced her head back up to meet Bridgett's sympathetic face.

"Can you blame them? The costs of supplies are all over the place. But, Charlie, you've got too many balls in the air to negotiate every deal. You can't keep operating as a one-woman show."

"I know." Charlotte raked her fingers through her hair. "My fear is they won't be satisfied with me hiring a CEO. They are going to want to install a stuffy board of directors or worse, make me take Truly public." She shuddered.

"You don't know that."

"It's a slippery slope." Charlotte took a gulp of her afternoon tea, hoping it would calm her. "Have you been able to vet any more candidates?"

Bridgett shuffled some papers on her desk. "The head-hunter came up with five more possibilities. Three of them look promising. But we could cast the net wider if you weren't so dead set against moving shop to the US."

Charlotte leaned back in her chair and stared up at the ceiling. She'd fled to London after the twins were born to carve out a future for herself, independent of the long shadow of her late father and the safety net of her brother and his new family. Truly You helped her do that. Owning and running a company gave her the self-worth she'd been searching for all her life.

Mostly.

Truly fed her mind and her creativity. Just not her heart. Even her libido was beginning to complain.

Damn Noah Hudson and his smoldering mouth.

She would relocate her business to Baltimore if he asked her to. Except he wasn't ever going to ask. Because she "wasn't his type." No matter how well their bodies fit together.

Heaving a frustrated sigh, she focused on the computer screen and her ever-patient sister-in-law. "Send me the resumés for the five names you have, and we can set something up."

Bridgett nodded just as Vivi appeared on the screen. She was dressed in her Blaze jersey, her dark braids adorned with ribbons in the team colors, red and black.

"Good morning, Sweet Pea," Charlotte gushed. "Looks like you are all set for another Spirit Friday at school."

"Mornin' Aunt Charlie. I miss you. When are you coming back?" Vivi demanded.

Charlotte's chest swelled at her niece's words. She'd been back in London for barely five days, and she missed the twins like crazy. Biologically, she was not the little girl's mother, but she'd carried her and her brother for nine months—she had the stretch marks to prove it. And she loved them as much as any mother could.

Yet another reason she had decamped to the other side of the Atlantic after giving birth. She wanted to give them time to bond as a family. And, if she were honest, it hurt not having the babies all to herself any longer.

She'd thought her maternal connection had waned a bit over the past five years. Given her visceral reaction to the little boy, Dalton, on Sunday, that wasn't the case. Just imagining enduring what those parents were going through had nearly knocked her on her ass in fear. If Noah hadn't been there to talk her down, she wasn't sure what she would have done.

Nope. As much as she wanted to be a part of her niece and nephew's lives, it was better to do it from afar. Like another continent afar.

"I'm not sure, honey," she replied. "But you know I'm always a video chat or phone call away."

Vivi's mouth formed a mulish line. "But you're asleep when we get home from school."

Guilty as charged.

"I'll tell you what," Charlotte said. "I'll wait up for you tonight. Call me after school and you can tell me whose jersey the kids are wearing."

"That's easy." Vivian's expression turned sour. "All the girls want Noah."

So does this girl.

"Go brush your teeth," Bridgett told her daughter. "And tell your brother we are leaving in ten minutes."

"Love you, Aunt Charlie," Vivi called out as she scurried off.

Charlotte blew her a kiss. "Love you more."

"This whole thing with Noah has taken on a life of its own," Bridgett remarked.

"What do you mean?" she asked, despite knowing precisely what her sister-in-law meant. London wasn't exactly the Moon. The social media chatter about her and Noah's supposed relationship had reached a fever pitch worldwide. Their theories bordered on ridiculous given that they both lived an ocean apart.

"The images of you two leaving the stadium Sunday," Bridgett said. "You looked . . . content. I'd even go so far as to say happy."

"I'm always happy," Charlotte argued.

"Uh, huh." Bridgett didn't look convinced.

"I am!"

"Okay, maybe happy is too generic of a word. Blissful would work." Bridgett snapped her fingers. "No. Enraptured. That accurately captions the look on your face in those images."

"Don't be silly. It's not at all what you think."

And there she went lying to her sister-in-law again. Charlotte was more than enraptured by Noah. Too bad he wasn't enraptured by her.

She's not my type. Not worth the effort.

The words he'd spoken three years ago still haunted her. Still rattled her confidence. Sure, they would burn up the sheets together. Their kisses assured her of that. But she wanted more from Noah. *More* that he very succinctly told her he wasn't ever going to give.

"Then what is it?" her sister-in-law prodded.

"Don't you have to get the kids to school?"

Bridgett rubbed her hands together. "I've got eight minutes. Spill."

Charlotte wasn't spilling anything. "Yeah, but you might want to get yourself ready. You know how catty those carpool moms can be if you're not looking your best."

She was being ridiculous. Bridgett was just as beautiful in sweatpants as she was in a power suit. And this morning she boasted the added rosy glow of a woman well-loved the night before.

Damn her.

She also wasn't falling for Charlotte's ploy. "There's more to this story, Charlie. If you don't want to talk about it with your family, that's fine. Just say so. Don't play us for fools."

It was no wonder Bridgett was a winning trial attorney. She played dirty.

"That's not what I'm trying to do," Charlotte told her. "Really, I'm simply helping him divert the negative press. He doesn't deserve it."

"Well, it's working. No one would dare say a disparaging thing about him now. Your Trulies would cancel them in a hot second." Bridgett leaned forward. "But the question is, why did you feel the need to jump in and lead the charge to avenge Noah? There's an entire department in the Blaze front office dedicated to handling that type of thing. Not to mention Noah's agent and his team."

As if they were all doing a bang-up job.

She couldn't very well tell her sister-in-law it was her fault Noah was being besieged by Bucky Kincaid and his band of muckrakers. That would require an explanation she didn't want to divulge. Mostly because her feelings for Noah were complicated.

And unrequited.

Charlotte was saved from the continued interrogation by Grayson's shriek.

"Momm-eee! I can't find my other shoe!"

Bridgett snapped her eyes shut. She looked like she was counting to ten.

"I'll let you go so you can deal with your domestic crisis." Charlotte reached for her mouse to end the call. "Don't forget to send me those resumés. I'll look over them tomorrow."

"This discussion isn't ov—"

She suppressed the twinge of guilt at cutting her sister-in-law off like that. What was over was this thing with Noah. There was no point in dissecting it. Not without alcohol involved, anyway.

Charlotte glided the cursor over to her email box, already dreading the urgent messages she knew had piled up during her thirty-minute phone call. Of course, there were twelve new ones. Her attention was drawn to one containing a Google alert about Noah. The fires would still be burning in the few minutes it took her to read whatever new article had been written about the Blaze quarterback. She clicked the link, smiling at the photo of him passing for a touchdown in Sunday's game.

The revelation he'd shared about his sister explained a lot about his personality. His stoic demeanor and soft-spoken character made a lot more sense knowing what she now did. Her heart ached for the little boy he'd been. He hadn't been the sick one, but he'd lost five years of a happy, normal life, nonetheless. Yet she was proud of the man he'd become. A man who didn't hesitate to rescue a stranger, asking nothing in return for his good deed.

The article was about the Blaze's upcoming game. It would be played in Pittsburgh, against their division rivals. Baltimore was predicted to win. The pundits were basing their analysis on Noah's much improved ability to read the playing field. Charlotte snorted.

"He could read the field last season," she said to her empty office. "It was the rest of the team that let him down."

Not anymore, though.

"Noah will be player of the week again this week and the Blaze will be two and O."

With that happy thought, she tackled the rest of her emails.

"DOES THAT BLOWHARD EVER SHUT UP?" Blaze tight end, Brody Janik, murmured to no one in particular. "I can't believe that asshole Kincaid has the balls to spew the lie that our loss was on you."

Sitting beside him at the bar in Devlin's, Noah assumed his teammate's question was rhetorical and didn't bother answering. As if Devlin's cantankerous opinions weren't enough, Brody, the senior member of the team's receiving corps had crashed tonight's dinner. Noah wasn't sure if the tight end's presence added anything to the painful post-mortem of Sunday's game. Still, he appreciated the support.

It had been four days since they'd lost to their division rivals, thanks to multiple dropped passes and the three interceptions Noah had thrown. It was as if he was living last season's nightmare all over again. Except this year, there was a horde of young girls and women wearing his jersey and screaming his name. Even though it was an away game.

Of course, the Pittsburgh players and fans didn't appreciate that fact one bit. And they'd let him know with their taunts and boos. The entire game had been a shitshow.

"None of those picks were his fault," Brody yelled at the television mounted above the bar. "I would have had one of those balls had I not been mauled by the cornerback. But did the zebras call it? Hell, no!"

Devlin slid a bowl of pretzels to the tight end. "Here, eat these. Your erratic blood sugar is making you cranky."

"If I'm cranky, it's because this dickhead is badmouthing

my QB for no good reason." Brody chucked a pretzel at the flat screen.

Devlin signaled to the bartender. "Change the channel to the Food Network before Kincaid causes everyone in the place to lose their appetite."

"You got it, boss." The bartender hunted for the remote. Not fast enough for the occupants of the bar to miss Bucky Kincaid's cockamamie theories, however.

"Of course, everyone in the world knows what is throwing Noah Dudson off his game." Kincaid smirked for the camera. "The guy can't perform—" Kincaid faked a cough "—without his woman cheering him on."

"Oh no, he didn't," Brody growled.

The bartender pointed the remote at the television.

"Don't," Noah snapped. He wanted to hear what the twit said before he had to read about it every time he picked up his phone.

"Ignore him, Hudson," Devlin said. "The guy is just tossing out click-bait."

Noah held up his hand. As much as he'd love to, no way was he ignoring this. Devlin sighed wearily as he shook his head.

Kincaid babbled on. "Which begs the question, where in the world is Princess Charlotte? I mean, she paid twenty-five thousand bucks to possess the Blaze quarterback. Every piece of him." The idiot winked at the screen. "Some would argue she overpaid." Kincaid raised his hand. "Of course, she probably has shoes that cost more than that. Either way, if these two really are an item, shouldn't she be in the stadium watching him play? Or has she given up on him just like I've been telling her brother's team they ought to do?"

"Is this guy for real?" Brody croaked out.

"Know what I think?" Kincaid asked his toady sidekick. "I

think the guy is just as big of a dud off the field, if you know what I mean."

Laughter echoed throughout Kincaid's set. Devlin snatched up the remote and changed the channel to the weather.

"Mother of God. How does that pompous shit get away with saying those things on television?" Brody demanded.

"It's a replay of his podcast," the bartender explained. "They give him a little more leeway there. The more outrageous he is, the more people tune in."

Brody stabbed at his phone screen. "I don't care. Slander is slander. Lucky for you, Huddy, my sister is a brilliant attorney. And married to the team's owner. She'll take your case pro-bono."

"I'm not suing the guy." Noah yanked the tight end's phone out of his hands and hit end call. "It would give Kincaid a bigger platform for his ego."

"Hudson's right. The weasel doesn't need a bigger megaphone." Devlin shot a look at Brody, gesturing to the tight end's phone in Noah's hand. "And you need to tighten your grip. No wonder that DB was able to wrench the ball away from you so easily."

Brody sputtered a protest that didn't register with Noah. He was too angry to think. His phone was already blowing up with calls from his agent. No doubt the guy wanted to get into a pissing match with Kincaid, too. Ignoring his phone, he tossed back what remained of his beer and stood. "I'm out of here."

Devlin stood, too, blocking the way. "Hudson, this loss is not on you, no matter what that loudmouth says. You executed the game plan exactly the way it was designed. You're not going to win every game. Put it out of your head and move on to this week's opponent."

It was ironic how much the former quarterback sounded like Noah's dad. He'd heard that same speech a million times before. The words were practical and true. Except they never quite wiped all the sting out of a loss.

"Yeah, Huddy," Brody added. "You have the support of everyone in our locker room. We win as a team. We lose as a team. You're too skilled of an athlete to be distracted by off-the-field chatter. Or a woman, no matter how hot she is." The tight end winked.

Devlin rolled his eyes. "Guess you aren't as skilled, then, because I remember you being very distracted by Shay."

"Hey! That's not how it was at all," Brody argued.

Noah left them to their good-natured bickering and headed for the exit. The thing was, Charlotte had become a major distraction. He resented how much headspace she took up. She was on his mind day and night.

Especially at night.

It was no surprise that he wanted her in his bed. A man would have to be dead not to. It was the idea of how much he wanted out of bed that was messing with his psyche.

The only time he could tune her out was when he was on the field. He'd spent years cultivating the skill of shutting off the extraneous noise when it mattered. Bucky Kincaid and his crowd of critics weren't even a whisper when the football was in Noah's hands.

Brody was right, though. Noah wasn't the problem. Still, he didn't want to throw shade at his receivers. They all caught his passes perfectly in practice. It was when the stands were full that they got the dropsies. He needed to work harder to make sure they got better at their craft.

Noah parked his truck in the garage of the modest townhouse he owned near the Blaze training facility and glanced down at his phone. It had been buzzing non-stop throughout the drive. He relaxed when a photo of his Meemaw popped up on the screen. He didn't dare ignore her.

"Hey there, gorgeous. What's up?"

"My blood pressure after watching that dang game on Sunday."

His grandmother didn't mince words. Nor did she believe in coddling. She'd been the one who had cared for Noah while his parents and sister traveled back and forth between Duke Medical Center and their small town in western North Carolina all those years. She was a no-nonsense woman who'd been widowed for longer than she was married.

Meemaw didn't believe in excuses, either. Beneath her gruff exterior, she had a heart of gold, however. And Noah credited her for every success he'd ever had. If his family were his rock, his grandmother was the boulder that centered them.

He tossed his keys into the ceramic bowl his niece made for him in vacation bible school this summer before heading to the fridge where he refilled his water bottle.

"I told you to stop watching those boys from Dallas," he teased. "They break your heart every year." His grandmother's greatest disappointment in life was that Noah hadn't been drafted by her favorite team.

Meemaw snorted. "Don't be smart with me, young man. You're not so big that I can't still tan your hide."

It was his turn to snort. Although, a small part of him didn't doubt the octogenarian's determination. If she wanted to lay a hand on Noah, she'd figure out a way to do it.

"It's a long season," he said, reciting the mantra of the week.

"Mmm. Tell that to that bully, Bucky Kincaid."

Noah grabbed the mail his cleaning lady had left on the counter and wandered into the family room, where he slid down onto the leather recliner that he'd paid an outrageous price for.

"Meemaw, I'm going to have dad cut off your cable if you keep tuning in to that idiot's show."

Noah's father had converted an old barn into a two-bedroom, two-bath home for his mother, complete with all the amenities she would need as she aged. The house was connected by a long breezeway to the home where Noah grew up. His grandmother had been living there for four years now and she didn't show any signs of needing the conveniences for elders any time soon.

"It never hurts to hear what people are sayin' about you. Even if most of it is a bunch of twaddle," she said. "Although I agree that your girlfriend could be a bit more supportive."

He banged the back of his head against the leather chair a few times. "I've already told you this. Charlotte Davis is not my girlfriend."

His grandmother made a disgruntled sound. "Nonsense. Pictures and videos don't lie, boy. That woman looks at you like you hung the moon. And your daddy still looks at your momma the way you were eying the princess. Don't even try to tell me there's nothing there."

There was plenty there. His junk grew tight just thinking about it. But even if he became a flashy superstar quarterback, he'd never be able to make a woman like Charlotte happy. She was playing in a different league. The attraction would fizzle eventually. His small-town world view would no longer be a novelty for her. She'd get bored. And that would be the unhappy end of it.

Noah had spent his life playing it cool, not making a scene, avoiding the drama while giving whatever he took on his all so as not to be a bother to his family. Or his teammates. He didn't like to let anyone down. And the thought of being a disappointment to Charlotte Davis was too much to consider.

He sighed. "What you're seeing is simple chemistry, that's all. Just two people attracted to one another."

"I hate to break it to you, Noah, but that's how most relationships start."

"We live on different continents." In different worlds.

"Pfft. What have I always told you about obstacles?"

"Every path has a few puddles. Sometimes you have to get your shoes wet," they both recited at the same time.

He smiled despite his mood. "The Atlantic Ocean is a pretty big puddle to wade through, Meemaw."

"So? Give her a reason to come back."

If only it was that simple.

For starters, he'd had the story all wrong for three years. She hadn't snuck out of his hotel room that night in London for the reasons he'd thought. Instead, she'd been protecting him. And then she'd come back. Noah scrubbed his hand down his face, embarrassed by the ugly things she'd overheard him say that day.

Christ, he deserved to be alone.

All this time, he'd thought she'd been conning him for his protection. That the woman he'd spent one of the best nights of his life with was an illusion. He'd believed she'd played him for a fool, saying what she thought he wanted to hear.

He'd been a fool, all right.

Charlotte hadn't been playacting with him any more than she had been with the little boy, Dalton, last week. Or when she'd confided to Noah about her lack of confidence. The woman he'd met and fallen for in London wasn't a mirage. He'd been angry at her all this time for no justifiable reason.

Or maybe he did have a good reason.

Self-preservation.

He couldn't fail her if he didn't try.

Meemaw rambled on. "The fans love that she's your good luck charm."

"Us losing on Sunday has nothing to do with Charlotte and me. You know that, right?"

"Of course, I do. And don't tell your daddy I said this, but football is only a game. Life, it's the real thing. And in twenty-eight years, I've never seen you look as content in your own skin as you did when you were looking into that woman's eyes." She sighed. "When you look at her, the weight of trying to shoulder all the burdens within this family or within your team is washed away. You've got to stop taking the blame for things that aren't your fault. Go find yourself something else to focus all your positive energy on. Or someone."

"I'm not sure I've got what it takes to hold on to a woman like her," he surprised himself by admitting.

"Pish posh. What does that even mean? You know how to treat a lady. You are kind and compassionate, with a great job and a college degree to fall back on when football ends. A catch by any woman's standards."

Except Charlotte Davis isn't any woman.

"Invite her to my birthday party next weekend," she insisted. "If it's just chemistry, she'll show her true feathers. Consider it your birthday gift for me. You never know. I'm getting up there in years. I've always wanted to meet a princess. This could be my last chance."

Was she serious right now?

The idea of Princess Charlotte accompanying him home to his rinky-dink town for any reason, much less a potluck birthday party for his grandmother at the VFW, was laughable. So why wasn't Noah laughing?

Because he wanted the happy ending, dammit. With

Charlotte. The question was, could she want one with him? Somehow, he doubted it.

"She's not an actual princess. That's just a nickname the tabloids gave her. And I told you a million times already, we are not a couple. Stop trying to guilt me into bringing her. You'll have to be satisfied with me showing up solo to your party."

She made a rumbling sound from deep in her throat. "Can I help it if I want to see my only grandson settled and happy?"

"I am happy." *Sort of.* "And you've got plenty of life left in you to see me settled."

"Says you!"

His chest tightened up. Was there something his grandmother wasn't telling him? His family wouldn't be holding back bad news because it was the football season, would they?

"Meemaw, is everything okay with you? Tell it to me straight or else I'm calling dad."

She huffed into the phone. "Everything is fine. I'm fit as a fiddle. Leave your dad out of this. He's already smothering me."

"He cares about you. We all do."

"If you care so much, see what you can do about throwing passes to your receivers so they can catch 'em. That'll be a nice birthday present for an old lady. Not as nice as meeting a princess, but as you say, it'll have to do."

He bit back a groan. Because really? His passes were landing right in the receivers' bread baskets. It wasn't his fault they couldn't hang on. But it was no use pleading his case with his grandmother. She never lost an argument.

"I'll do my best."

NINE

UNFORTUNATELY, his best wasn't good enough.

The plane ride from Arizona back to Baltimore that Sunday night was quiet. Mainly because the Blaze had dropped another game. Thankfully, the blame for this one could be laid squarely at the feet of their kicker. Noah had perfectly executed three long passes down the field to get them in scoring position with only three ticks left on the game clock—only to have the field goal bounce off the left upright.

To be fair, one of Arizona's players got his paw on the ball as it passed over the line of scrimmage. Otherwise, Taylor's kick would have given them a walk-off victory. Still, Noah was relieved not to be the scapegoat for this one.

Beside him, Brody Janik chuckled as he scrolled through his phone.

"You've got to hand it to Charlotte's devotees," the tight end said. "They've got your back."

Noah shot him a *what's that supposed to mean* look.

Brody chortled again. "Except in this case, they are circling the wagons around Taylor." He leaned over so Noah could see his phone screen. "They are coming to his defense for missing the field goal. They've even started a campaign asking fans to donate to his anti-bullying charity. They're each giving nine bucks to match his number. So far, they've raised nearly ten K and it's only been two hours."

Sure enough, Charlotte's Trulies were all over social media in support of Taylor and the Blaze. Noah's chest squeezed with pride at the devoted way people stood with Charlotte. She deserved it. If only she had the same confidence about her abilities.

"It's a nice gesture," he admitted. "I have no doubt Bucky Kincaid will find a way to taint it somehow, though."

"I'd like to see the asshole try," Brody squeezed out through his tight jaw.

"He'd be a fool to mess with Charlie's fans," Jay McManus said, appearing out of nowhere to stand in the aisle next to Brody's seat. "They're already coming for him about his remarks last week."

"See? What did I tell ya?" Brody looked between Noah and his brother-in-law. "I suggested Huddy hire Bridgett to sue the guy for slander." He rubbed his hands together. "But this will be infinitely more fun to watch play out."

Noah didn't bother commenting. He was too busy trying to quash the unease rolling through his gut. The Blaze owner rarely made a social call to the back of the team plane. And since they'd just lost a tough one, Noah doubted it was to deliver an "atta-boy" to anyone.

"Switch seats with me," McManus demanded of Brody.

Any other player would be halfway to the front of the plane by now, but Brody's relationship with the Blaze owner was unique. The tight end hesitated, almost as if McManus' words had been a request.

"Are you asking as the boss man or my brother-in-law?" he eventually drawled.

A charged stalemate followed until Brody rolled his eyes and hastily unfastened his seatbelt.

"I really don't know what my sister sees in you," he said, hauling himself out of his seat and shoulder checking McManus on his way past.

"Don't eat all the cookies up there. I don't need to explain to my wife why you ended up in a sugar coma," McManus warned Brody.

The tight end gave a backward wave that might have included an obscene gesture before he walked away.

The Blaze owner sighed heavily as he settled into the seat Brody had just vacated. The seatbelt clicked loudly in the quiet night.

So much for the guy only staying for a minute.

McManus rested his head against the seatback and closed his eyes. The moment stretched painfully before he spoke.

"You played a hell of a game tonight."

Hmm. Maybe there were "atta-boys" for a loss.

Noah remained silent. There was no point in responding with a thank you. The guy was paying him to play a "hell of a game" every time he stepped onto the field.

McManus raised his lids enough to give Noah the side-eye. Apparently, silence wasn't going to cut it here.

"Everyone played well today. We win as a team. We lose as a team." Noah parroted Brody's words from the other night.

"And you're the ultimate team player," McManus replied.

Noah let the comment pass, waiting to see where his boss went with it. If he even meant it as a compliment.

McManus' eyes were open wide now. And laser focused on Noah. "But right now, I need you to drop the 'never kiss and tell' act and tell me why Bucky Kincaid has it out for you. And what role does Charlotte play in this?"

Ahh, there it is. The real reason for this little visit.

Charlotte's brother was a brilliant, self-made billionaire. It didn't surprise Noah that he'd finally put some of the puzzle pieces together. It pissed him off that McManus would somehow want to lay any blame on his sister, though.

"Charlotte's not responsible for any of the bullshit that comes out of Kincaid's mouth," Noah snapped, not giving a damn that this was the man who signed his paychecks.

The corners of the other man's mouth twitched slightly. "Your defense of my sister is admirable. I respect that. I respect it a lot." His shoulders relaxed. "Her championing of you yesterday was equally emphatic."

Her what?

The Blaze owner's smile turned sly. "She beat Brody to the punch, insisting that Bridgett file a slander suit. Too bad for her. The team had already stolen her thunder and threatened one of our own. Not to mention filing a formal complaint against the network and a few choice emails to the show's sponsors." He glanced at his watch. "Right about now, Kincaid ought to be making an on-air apology for his salacious remarks. I demanded they send us each a video copy. It should land in your email inbox when we are wheels down." McManus chuckled. "It might have been a harsher punishment to let Charlotte's Trulies handle it, though." His face sobered. "He'll know now not to mess with my sister's reputation. Or that of my franchise quarterback."

Noah swallowed roughly. No one on the team had ever mentioned the franchise tag. As far as he knew, he was fighting for his life on the Blaze. It was a heady thought, knowing management was still behind him.

He decided to throw his boss a bone.

"Kincaid made the moves on Charlotte, and she turned him down. He didn't like it."

McManus' jaw clicked loudly. "And you somehow came to her rescue?"

"Yes." The one word would have to suffice because Noah wasn't sharing the details of the rest of that night with anyone.

"Charlotte returned the favor by rescuing you at the auction."

Noah nodded. "I supposed that kiss plastered all over social media was her way of thanking you too?"

A twinge of guilt lodged itself in Noah's gut. He had been the one to initiate that kiss. Still, it was safer to keep steering along the "no comment" route.

McManus sighed heavily. "And tonight? Do you think Kincaid will let it drop with his apology?"

"He'd be a fool not to."

The Blaze owner barked out a laugh. "The world is full of fools. Especially those who are constantly chasing fame."

"Charlotte is lucky she has you for a brother and protector, then."

A soft smile appeared on McManus' mouth. "My sister is—"

"Extraordinary." The word slipped out before Noah could stop it.

McManus stilled in his seat. His shrewd gaze pinned Noah to his seatback. "That she is," he said, his tone thoughtful. "Not everyone gets close enough to see that about her."

"The world is full of fools," Noah repeated.

"Mm. My sister is lucky to also have you in her life."

I'm not in her life, he wanted to scream. At least not the way he wanted to be.

The seatbelt clicked again when McManus unfastened it. He groaned slightly as he unfurled his tall body from the seat. "Although maybe keep the PDA off social media. My daughter has a massive crush on you. The last thing I need is more tension between the women in my life."

Great.

McManus paused before making his way back up front. "She'd do well to end up with a guy like you."

The comment stunned Noah.

"I'm referring to Charlotte, by the way," McManus clarified. "No one will ever be good enough for my daughter."

"YOU'VE GOT to be kidding me!" Charlotte barely resisted the urge to toss her morning coffee at her computer screen. Only because that slimeball, Bucky Kincaid, wouldn't feel a thing if she did. "That wasn't an apology. That was a 'boys will be boys' cop-out if I ever heard one."

"Mm-hmm, we call that a 'word salad' in court," Bridgett murmured over her cellphone.

"And does he think anyone's buying his BS about it all just being 'locker room smack talk?' That he was trying to 'psych Noah up to play better?' I can't believe the network let him get away with that."

"He brings in big numbers," Bridgett replied. "And eyes on the screen translate to big money. They look the other way and line their pockets even when what he says straddles the line."

Charlotte groaned in frustration. "And that whole part where he apologizes to Noah and offers to go grab a beer with him—ugh! I won't be able to keep food down for a week."

Bridgett chuckled. "I doubt the two will be bonding over a beer any time soon."

"Yeah. I don't see Noah taking the bait."

That didn't mean guilt wasn't gnawing at her stomach. If

she hadn't dragged him onto Bucky Kincaid's radar three years ago, Noah wouldn't have to be constantly watching his back. He wouldn't have to worry that everything he did could turn into fodder for social media trolls. And then she'd gone and made matters worse when she "bought" Noah at the auction.

"Do you think this will be the end of it?" she asked Bridgett.

Her sister-in-law shook her head. "Bucky has a target on his back. If he's smart, he'll tread carefully. He has to know he won't get a second chance with Jay. Or your Trulies."

Charlotte had to smile at the effusive way her fans had come for Bucky after his show on Friday. And how they'd lifted the Blaze placekicker following yesterday's game. Blaze fans brushed off the missed field goal, even going so far as to contribute to the guy's charity which was now a hundred thousand dollars richer .

"Listen, Charlie, that's not why I called," Bridgett said. "Your lenders are thrilled with your CEO selection."

At least someone is.

Charlotte silently chastised herself for the thought. The woman she'd chosen came with impeccable credentials, a proven track record leading a successful retailer in the U.S., and no hesitation about relocating to London. By all accounts, she was fair-minded and likeable. And she didn't balk when Charlotte insisted that she remain in the loop on the day-to-day operations.

"But they still want you to seriously consider taking the company public," Bridgett added with a rush.

As if this day could get any worse.

Charlotte's heart sank. It was her worst fear confirmed. Taking her company public meant appointing a board of directors. Yet another layer between her and the enterprise she'd created from scratch. The one thing that belonged to her and only her.

For now, anyway.

Bridgett sighed on the other end of the phone. "Look, they've only mentioned that you consider it. Nothing has to happen in the short-term. In the meantime, I think we should get it out there in front of the media and other potential investors that you've taken the step of bringing in someone to help you strengthen your brand. It may calm the waters, so to speak."

Ha! What about my fears? What's going to calm them?

Why was it that every time she was searching for her inner calm, Noah's face appeared? His brown eyes instilling confidence. His fingers feathering down her cheek. His full lips murmuring reassuring words.

You're a smart woman. Trust your instincts.

Noah believed in her. More than she believed in herself.

Hire someone to teach you the skills, he had advised.

Hadn't she just done that? The lenders could "suggest" she take Truly You public all they wanted. Before it came to that, however, Charlotte was going to learn everything she could about running her own business.

"You're right," Charlotte agreed. "A little schmoozing of the media never hurts. Let's finalize the deal with her and set up a press conference for early next week."

"It might be hard to get everyone over to London by then." Bridgett sounded surprised. Probably because she didn't expect Charlotte to agree so readily. "Your new CEO has to make some plans for her move and the Blaze are playing on Thursday night. I couldn't get to London until the weekend."

"Then I'll come to you. We'll make the big announcement next Tuesday."

It was a great excuse to see the twins.

And possibly a football game.

THE BLAZE LOCKER room was bumping following their dominating win that Thursday night.

"Hell of a game in front of a national TV audience, fellas." The Blaze head coach commended his team while pacing up and down the center of the room, his players and assistant coaches forming an oval around him. "Give it up for our defense! They played lights out football, holding them to only three points." He tossed a ball to the defensive captain. "You guys were beasts. Everyone on the D gets a game ball."

A chorus of whoops and cheers echoed throughout the room. Noah clapped along with his teammates. He'd had a great game, but the defense took it to another level tonight. They were the stars of the show.

One of the position coaches tossed Coach another ball. "And let's not forget about our offense. They played precision football, putting thirty-four points on the board with no turnovers and not a single dropped pass." Coach turned toward Noah. "Excellent job navigating through their tough defense, Hudson."

A wolf whistle rang out.

"He was on his game tonight because his woman was in the stadium," someone shouted.

Christ.

Noah ground his back teeth together. He'd had no idea Charlotte was back in Baltimore. Not until he saw her on the Jumbotron after his second touchdown pass. The crowd had roared with delight as she clapped and high-fived everyone in the owner's suite. The sight of her jubilant smile made the breath hang up in his lungs for several heartbeats. Until he realized she wasn't here for him. She was like any other Blaze fan, cheering for her brother's team. Plain and simple. Social media, his teammates, the fans may think otherwise, but Noah knew the truth.

And, dammit, he hated that truth. His jaw clenched when several of his teammates chimed in with their own ridiculous comments.

"She's our lucky charm," one guy called out.

"Yeah, Huddy, we're two and O when the boss' sister shows up to cheer you on. Whatever you do, don't do her wrong. I want a championship ring again," the team's center added, and the rest of the locker room hooted in agreement.

Coach's smile was chagrined. "Okay, knock it off. We won today because we played to our potential. We do that every time we take the field, and we'll be in that championship game, no problem." He glanced around the room. "Now, where's Taylor? He scored ten of our points with his kicking foot today. He gets this game ball for not losing his mojo after last week."

Taylor stepped forward to receive his ball. "Thanks to the Trulies for keeping the fans from running me out of town," he quipped.

"That's what I'm talking 'bout! Princess Charlotte brings the good mojo all around," the center responded.

"Enjoy your weekend off, fellas," Coach was saying. "See you all Monday morning."

Noah made a beeline for the showers, hoping the media would focus on reviewing the game at the post-game presser.

They didn't.

After the fourth question intimating that he played better when Charlotte was in the stadium, Noah shot a death glare at Asia. The Blaze media director was quick to come to his rescue.

"If there's nothing else about the specifics of this evening's game, we are going to adjourn for the night. Thank you, Noah," Asia said as he slipped out of the press room and into the deserted hallway housing the training rooms.

He blew out an annoyed breath. *How had things gotten so effed up?* When he sucked, that's all the media wanted to talk about. Now, when his passer rating was the second highest in the league, all they wanted to focus on was Charlotte Davis. And the torrid love affair everyone assumed they were having.

In his dreams.

He rounded the corner, only to collide with someone walking toward him. Except it wasn't someone. It was her. As if he'd conjured her up somehow.

"Oh," Charlotte gasped against his chest.

Noah groaned as he breathed in a lungful of her unique scent. His fingers glided along the soft cashmere of her sweater, one hand sliding down to manacle her wrist. Before he knew what he was doing, he'd tugged her into one of the empty training rooms. He kicked the door closed with his foot, then did a one-eighty, pressing Charlotte's back against the wall, boxing her in with his hands on either side of her head.

His breath was sawing through his lungs as he studied her up close. How had he not noticed her lashes were a deep auburn instead of brown? Or that she had a little scar just above her right eyebrow, probably from a fall as a child. His chest ached at the thought of her being hurt. He resisted the urge to press his lips to the white mark.

"Hi," she whispered, breaking the charged silence.

Noah didn't trust his voice. Instead, he kept his mouth shut and continued to catalog the intricacies of her beautiful face.

"I was looking for you."

That got his attention. His gaze collided with hers. She sunk her teeth into her bottom lip, drawing his gaze down to her tempting mouth. The move had him swallowing a groan.

"Vivian drew you a picture," she murmured. "It's a school night, so she wasn't allowed to come to the game. I said I'd give it to you."

She reached down to her purse sandwiched between them. Her hand grazed his stomach, making them both flinch. Noah hissed. Her eyes went round when he leaned in, trapping her hand against his abdomen.

"You are not the reason we won tonight," he ground out.

Charlotte looked at him, her expression a mix of shock and annoyance. "No. Of course not." She shook her head. "Your receivers didn't drop your passes. I had nothing to do with it."

He nodded, his chin nearly connecting with hers. "I don't need you in the stadium cheering for me in order to play well, you hear me?"

"You don't." She gave her head another slight shake before jerking her chin up. "And who says I came to the game tonight because of you?"

Her sassy tone snapped what remained of Noah's self-control. Without conscious thought, his fingers were tunneling through her luscious hair, angling her head just so before he crushed her mouth with his. Charlotte responded with a seductive sigh. The sound drove him even wilder. Teeth and tongues collided as he plundered her mouth.

Charlotte should have objected to the rough way he was handling her. Any woman should. His mother would be appalled.

Instead, she let him have his way, formfitting her body against his. His junk grew unbearably tight at the contact. She managed to work free the hand trapped beneath their bodies, trailing it up his chest to cradle his jaw. He wanted to beg her to take her hand in the other direction, but he didn't dare tear his mouth away. It appeased him slightly when her other hand slipped beneath his sweatshirt, where she traced soothing circles along the skin of his back.

If it was her intent to calm him down, she was going about it the wrong way. Her simple touch ignited all the nerve endings in his body. She moaned when he eased his thigh between hers. He echoed the sound when his fingers snaked beneath her cropped sweater, coming in contact with the soft skin of her belly. The circles on his back became more agitated as her nails took over.

He was in the midst of hiking up one of her legs around his waist when the door burst open.

"There you are," Brody exclaimed as he bounded into the room.

"Christ, Brody! Don't you know how to knock?" Noah snapped, trying to shield Charlotte from view.

"Hey, dude. I didn't expect you to be hiding in the training room playing Seven Minutes in Heaven." Brody shot Charlotte one of his toothpaste ad grins. "I knew there was something going on between you two."

Noah resisted the urge to throttle his most reliable receiver. "Was there something you needed?"

The tight end grew serious. "Your phone has been

buzzing nonstop. I wasn't trying to be nosy. It buzzed itself right off the shelf of your locker." He handed the phone to Noah. "You've missed ten calls from your dad."

A chill ran up his spine. His dad knew the post-game routine. He wouldn't call unless it was important. He slid his finger to the voicemail button and listened.

"Everything okay?" Brody asked a moment later.

"No." Noah swiped to his favorites screen. "My grandmother is in the hospital."

"Meemaw?" There was a hint of panic in Charlotte's voice. As if she and his formidable grandmother were fast friends or something.

"The one and only." He punched at his father's contact.

He answered before the phone even rang. "Son."

"Dad." Noah dragged his fingers through his hair. "How is she?"

"She's stable," his father answered. "They're still running tests. The doctors want to keep her overnight."

"What happened?"

"We were watching the game when she became light-headed and nearly passed out."

"I did no such thing," Meemaw shouted in the background.

His father swore. "She's so bullheaded, she won't let them give her anything to help her rest."

"That stuff will make me too groggy for Silver Sneakers tomorrow. I can't have that Marcy Kuttner beating my mall-walking time."

There was never a doubt where Noah got his competitiveness from.

"You aren't going to Silver Sneakers tomorrow," his father said, showing more patience with his mother than usual. "Not until we know what caused this episode."

"I'm a soon-to-be eighty-five-year-old woman. That's what caused this episode, as you call it. Now let me talk to my grandson."

His father's sigh was a weary one. "Tell her to behave, Noah."

"Nice game," Meemaw said when she got her hands on the phone. She sounded tired, but that was to be expected. It was closing in on midnight. "I see your princess came back from London."

"For crying out loud, Meemaw. Not this again." He pinched the bridge of his nose. "Why don't you focus on doing what the medical staff tell you to do so we can all celebrate your birthday this weekend. I'll be home first thing in the morning. If you're good, I'll take you to DQ for lunch."

"I'll promise to be good if you promise to bring your girlfriend with you."

"Meemaw, we talked about this—"

His grandmother moaned. "My head is starting to spin again. I should probably stop yapping and get some rest if I want to enjoy my birthday party this weekend. It could be my last, you know."

She ended the call before he could talk to his dad.

Christ.

The woman was incorrigible.

But she's also not getting any younger. *What if this is her last birthday?*

Noah swore as he pocketed his phone. Brody and Charlotte looked at him with concern.

"She's fine," he told them. "Just ornery."

A fond smile formed on Brody's mouth. "My grandpa Gus was like that. Annoying as hell. What I wouldn't give to have one more conversation with him, though." He looked between Charlotte and Noah. "Alrighty then. I'll let you two get back to . . . whatever it was that you were doing." He shot Noah a cat-ate-the-canary grin. "But you've got some 'splaining to do when I see you next." He backed out of the door with a bow before closing them inside the training room.

Charlotte rolled her eyes at Brody's antics before refocusing them on Noah.

"I'm glad she's okay," she said.

"Mmm."

Her teeth found her bottom lip again as she studied him for a long moment. With a sigh, she dug her hand into the bag slung over her shoulder and pulled out a folded piece of pink construction paper.

"From Vivian."

She placed it on the training table between them and turned to leave.

"Charlotte."

One eyebrow shot up in question when she looked back over her shoulder at him.

"Remember that favor I did for you in London?"

She jerked her chin up and down.

"Good. Because I'm going to need you to help me out this weekend."

THE EARLY MORNING flight was rowdy, surprisingly. A crowd of college students and alumni were headed to Asheville for a football game. Noah and Charlotte tried to remain as inconspicuous as possible, hanging back as everyone else boarded, before taking the first two seats in First Class.

"This is really all you brought?" he asked as he hefted her carryon into the overhead bin.

Charlotte slid into the window seat. "You keep asking

that. You told me we were going to a high school football game and a family party for your grandmother's birthday. Were you expecting me to bring a trunk full of ball gowns and designer shoes to wear to both?"

She hated how waspish she sounded. But she was tiring of him treating her like the high maintenance princess everyone assumed her to be. Especially since he should know better by now.

It didn't help that she was operating on very little sleep, either, after spending the night tossing and turning, reliving their steamy interlude in the training room. She shouldn't have agreed to this. What was she thinking spending a weekend with a man who could turn it on and off at will? One minute, he had her melting in his arms. The next minute, he was succinctly explaining that she "owed him" and he needed her to join him in North Carolina for the weekend to pay off her debt.

Sighing, he sat down beside her. "I only meant that I've never traveled with a woman who packed so economically, that's all."

Well.

It was a back-handed compliment, but she'd take it. And that was not jealousy bubbling up in her chest. He'd enjoyed a few romantic getaways with other women before. So what?

Except this was most assuredly not a romantic getaway. He'd made that fact perfectly clear last night when he told her she was coming along because his Meemaw wanted to meet her.

You're not his type, remember?

"So how is this going to work?" she demanded when the plane was taxiing down the runway. "The whole world thinks we are an item. Are we pretending in front of your family?"

He gave her a pointed look. "I don't lie to the people who

matter the most to me. My family is everything. I've told them we're just friends."

Charlotte huffed. "Do you always kiss your friends like you're the last two people on Earth?"

Holy hell, she needed coffee. *Or duct tape.*

His eyes darkened as his gaze drifted to her lips. The plane lurched before banking sharply left. She slammed her eyes shut. As much to avoid his penetrating gaze as to keep her equilibrium while the plane made its ascent.

Noah's fingers found hers on the arm rest. He gave her hand a reassuring squeeze. She squeezed back.

"I don't know what we are," he said once the plane leveled out. "But you can always count on me."

Tears pressed at the back of her eyes. Damn, she was tired. Tired of never being enough. Never being the right one. The right type.

Especially since he'd acted like she was his type last night. And the other times he'd kissed her. In fact, she'd never felt more like a man's type. For some reason, the pigheaded guy next to her refused to see it.

No matter. She'd be his type for the weekend. His "friend-zone" type. It was the least she could do for continually dragging him into her messy life. Later, she'd worry about the repeated hits her heart was about to take these next few days.

ELEVEN

NOAH TOOK it as a sign of good luck that they managed to make it through the Asheville airport without a camera being shoved in their faces. Not that anyone had a chance to. He set a pretty fast pace as they hurried from the plane to the kiss and ride. Fortunately, Charlotte's long legs matched him stride for stride.

He really needed to stop fixating on those damn long legs of hers. Sleep had been impossible last night. Not when all he could think about was her legs wrapped around his waist while he lost himself inside of her.

Christ.

This was a dumbass play. Spending the weekend with a woman he couldn't keep his hands off of. Inviting her into his inner sanctum. Letting her see the real Noah Hudson, in all his simple glory. Well, better now than later. This way, it wouldn't hurt too much when she realized she preferred worldly playboys to small town jocks.

"Yoo-hoo!"

Noah froze at the sound of the familiar voice. Charlotte stopped short behind him.

"Noah! Over here!" A horn honked.

"I think the woman in the minivan is trying to get your attention," Charlotte deadpanned.

He pinned her with a look. "Ya think?"

It was too late for second thoughts. Charlotte was here now. Less than half a football field away from his sister and his two little nieces. The horn honked again.

"Brace yourself," he warned her before trudging toward the minivan idling by the curb.

Squeals of "Uncle Noah" floated through the passenger window. Alex shushed her daughters before racing out of the driver's door and around the hood of the van so she could throw her arms around him. Her enthusiasm was over the top. More suited for a guy who'd just returned from a year's deployment overseas. Not a brother she'd seen in person a month earlier.

"Hey, you! What a game you had last night."

His nieces were chanting his name, accompanied by the pounding of their fists and feet in their car seats.

"What are you doing here?" he asked. "I thought mom was picking me up."

Alex's brown eyes sparkled with mischief. She brushed her long blonde hair back from her face. She'd kept it long once it had grown back, explaining to Noah once that her hair was a badge of honor as a cancer survivor. And motivation for the young patients she cared for. The only time she pulled it into a ponytail was when she was working a shift at the hospital.

"The girls and I were packed up and on the road from Winston-Salem earlier than I expected. Chris decided to come down separately after his morning meetings." She bounced up on her toes. "I offered to swing by and grab you since Dad spent most of the night at the hospital. Mom is taking Meemaw home as we speak. The tests were all negative for anything major, by the way. She was dehydrated." His sister peeked past his shoulder at the woman standing behind him. "And I'm not gonna lie. I was dying to meet your guest."

Charlotte extended her hand to Alex. His sister had her wrapped up in a hug before Noah could warn her a handshake wasn't going to cut it.

"Alex, this is Charlotte Davis." Noah grabbed Charlotte's carryon and rolled both their bags to the rear of the van. "Charlotte, this is my sister, Alex. The two little darlings in the car are my nieces, Maisy and Ainsley."

"Oh my gosh," his sister gushed. "I can't believe I'm actually meeting you. I'm a huge fan of your products." She twisted her wrist several times, showing off her armful of silver bracelets. "I love the affirmation bracelets the best. I give them out to all the patients on my floor. The kids need all the inspo they can get, right?"

"Um, yes. Yes, they do." Charlotte aimed a WTF look in his direction.

"My sister is a nurse at the children's hospital," Noah explained.

"Seriously?" Alex slapped him on the shoulder. "You didn't tell her anything about us, did you?" She heaved an exasperated sigh before rolling her eyes at Charlotte. "He's like a fortress, this one. He doesn't share anything."

"I can attest to that." Charlotte shot him a mocking smile.

Alex opened the van's sliding door and his niece's squeals rained out over the kiss and ride.

"Uncle Noah!"

"Hey you two troublemakers. Did you save any of those animal crackers for me?"

"I'll sit with the girls," Charlotte surprised him by saying. "There's no way your long legs will fit back there."

"More like you don't want to spend forty minutes being interrogated by my sister, huh?" he murmured as he helped her into the car.

She tossed another one of those taunting grins over her shoulder. "And let you miss out on all the fun?"

Damn, there was so much to this woman that he appreciated. Her snark was just part of her appeal. The vision of her jean-clad ass swaying in front of his face was also fascinating. He slammed the door shut and jumped into the passenger seat before he did something stupid, like joining her in the backseat just so he could hold her hand again.

"Who is Maisy and who is Ainsley?" Charlotte asked his nieces as Alex pulled away from the airport.

"I'm Maisy," the four-year-old replied. "Are you really a princess?"

Noah groaned. *Here we go.*

"Sometimes," Charlotte told them. "But only in my imagination."

He laughed out loud at that one.

She raised her voice to be heard over him. "Every girl should think of herself as a princess. That way, you always have the right amount of confidence to do and be anything you want. That's important when you want people to take you seriously."

"Amen, sister," Alex chimed in as she merged onto the highway.

Noah met Charlotte's eyes in the extra rearview mirror Alex used to keep an eye on the kids. He wanted to ask her why she didn't believe that to be true for herself. Why she doubted her capabilities when she'd already proven herself to be a shrewd businesswoman?

Maisy beat him with a follow-up question of her own. "Do we call you Aunt Charlotte?"

Christ.

He speared his sister with a pointed look. Alex barely managed to stifle a giggle before she shrugged.

"Why don't you call me Charlie," Charlotte said. "That's what my family calls me."

Noah's body instantly ached as though he'd been hit in the chest with a helmet.

That's what my family calls me.

They weren't her family. Charlotte would likely never see his nieces again after this weekend. It felt too intimate for his nieces to call her by her nickname.

It also felt right.

So fucking right.

He risked another glance back. Ainsley's head was already bobbing to the side as the two-year-old drifted off to sleep. Maisy was regaling Charlotte about her friend whose guinea pig was also named Charlie. Charlotte smiled adoringly at everything his niece said.

For a reputed pampered society princess, she had no problem going one-on-one with kids. He'd noticed that the day she'd interacted with Dalton and his family. Her interest was genuine. Her concern was real. All he had to do was remember those moments in the elevator when she nearly passed out imagining her niece or nephew suffering through what Dalton had.

"Mm-hmm."

His sister's muttering had his attention shifting.

"What?" he demanded when she aimed a knowing smile in his direction.

I love her, Alex mouthed.

"Shut up and drive."

Alex laughed loudly this time as Noah focused on the familiar mountains rising ahead of them. Better to concentrate on something concrete than the crazy feelings churning deep in his gut. Especially since he was pretty sure he'd fallen in love with Charlotte Davis three years ago in a London hotel room, talking the night away, munching on crisps and falling asleep to a decades-old chick flick.

He was so screwed.

FORTY-FIVE MINUTES LATER, Alex exited the highway onto the main drag through his little hometown. Like one of Pavlov's dogs, Maisy began chirping about lunch at DQ.

"No DQ today," Alex told her. "You'll have plenty of junk food at the football game tonight."

"But Mommmmm," Maisy wailed as the DQ came into view.

Noah did a double take at the ice cream store's marquee, declaring today as "Noah Hudson Day." The marquees for the bank and the Tractor Supply announced the same thing.

"What the hell is Noah Hudson Day?" He looked over at his sister.

Alex sported a huge grin. "Surprise!"

Maisy echoed her mother. "Surprise, Uncle Noah! We get to wear your jersey to the game tonight. The one from when Gramps was your coach."

Noah's teeth began to hurt, his jaw was clenched so tight. "Alex?"

"You didn't think you were coming home just for Meemaw's birthday, did you?"

"Uh, yeah, I did."

His sister imitated her daughters and bounced in her seat. "Then it's the perfect surprise."

"Dammit, Alex," he growled. "I hate surprises."

"I know. That's what makes this one so much fun." She took pity on him. "They are renaming the football stadium in your honor tonight."

What the actual fuck?

"No one asked me if they could do that."

"Because you would have said no. You're way too modest, by the way. It's happening though, little brother. Face it. You're the biggest star to come out of our football program. The whole county is turning out for the ceremony tonight."

When they rounded the corner leading up to the home where he'd grown up, Noah spotted a convoy of television vans parked outside the post office. His gut clenched.

"Don't tell me the media is covering this?"

"Of course they are, silly. Lest you forget, stuff like this is big news in small towns."

Noah whipped his head around to stare at Charlotte. Her expression was unreadable—except for her teeth buried in her bottom lip. Dammit. What had he dragged her into?

THEY DROVE DOWN A LONGISH DRIVEWAY, ending at a sprawling brick rambler with a wraparound porch featuring Chippendale railings. It was all decked out with pumpkins, a buffalo plaid mat and other fall decorations. All of that paled compared to the splendor that was behind the home, however, an unobstructed view of the Blue Ridge Mountains in all their autumnal glory. Charlotte was trying to take it all in when Noah yanked her from the van.

"You don't have to stay," he said, his words a hurried whisper.

His brown eyes held a look of raw anguish. He hadn't counted on them being seen together by the paps. This trip was so under the radar, they'd both decided she didn't need any security.

Cleary, he didn't want to add any more fuel to the rumors of their relationship. She got that. She hated that it was because he didn't believe she was his type. But that was neither here nor there. Their reality was a football game swarming with cameras.

Noah's voice wasn't as steady as usual. She had no doubt that if he had a way of leaving, too, he would use it. Humble didn't even begin to describe this man. Which was so incongruous with every professional athlete she'd ever known. His reticence only made him even more endearing.

You can always count on me, he'd confessed to her on the plane.

Well, that went ditto for her. They were in this together. For better or for worse.

Her heart stuttered a beat at her brain's whimsical choice of words. She patted him on the chest, letting her palm linger over his heart a moment longer for added reassurance. His heartbeat stuttered for a few beats as well. Their gazes collided and held.

"You're leaving?"

Maisy's question had Charlotte dropping her hand and turning to placate the little girl. She fingered the end of one of Maisy's braids.

"I'm not going anywhere, Miss Maisy. I've never been to a high school football game. And you promised there would be funnel cakes."

"Yay!" Maisy raced to the front porch.

Noah remained where he was. "You sure?"

She nodded with more conviction than she felt. "I owe you, remember?"

He closed his eyes with a pained sigh. "I was wrong to ask this of you."

"Why *did* you bring me here, Noah?"

Charlotte was surprised at the steady way she'd voiced the question, considering how desperately she wanted to know his answer. He'd told her she was here at his grandmother's request. She knew there wasn't anything he wouldn't do for his Meemaw. Deep down, though, she hoped she was here for a different reason.

His lashes jerked up, revealing a maelstrom of emotion in his eyes. Just when she thought he might answer, his sister called to them from the porch.

"Hey, you two. Lunch is on the table. Come and get it."

MEEMAW WAS everything Charlotte expected and, yet, so much more. For starters, the older woman's eyes were bright and discerning, even after a night spent in the hospital. Her grey hair was long, its sleek waves framing her face. Most women of her age favored a shorter style. Noah hadn't exaggerated her height—six feet, if Charlotte had to guess. Meemaw still carried herself with the regality of an aristocrat, shoulders back, chin held high.

An aristocrat who drove a giant pickup truck.

"Do you mind if I borrow your truck this afternoon, Meemaw?" Noah asked during lunch.

"You're welcome to use my van," Alex offered as she nabbed a pickle from Ainsley's hand before it landed on the floor.

Noah shot his sister a horrified look.

Their mother, Val, chuckled. "It's your brother's day. Let

him drive something that isn't a mom-mobile." She turned to Noah. "Are you going to show Charlotte around town?"

He gave Charlotte a sheepish look. "Actually, I was going to head over to the high school. See what I can do to dial back this whole Noah Hudson Day nonsense."

"It's not nonsense and you'll do no such thing," Meemaw declared, lowering her palm to the tabletop with a loud whack.

Noah sighed. "This weekend is supposed to be a celebration for you, Meemaw. Not me."

"And what if honoring your many accomplishments is what I want for my birthday, huh?"

"Check mate," Charlotte mumbled so that only Noah would hear.

He smacked her thigh with his. She nudged hers against his in response. Their nonverbal sparring continued back and forth until Noah placed a hand on her thigh.

And left it there.

She tried to jerk her leg away, but he spread out his long fingers and anchored her leg where it was. His lips turned up slightly at the corners as he shoveled some potato chips into his mouth with his free hand. Charlotte stole the last chip off his plate in retaliation.

"Hey!" He tried to grab it back.

"Mm," she said as she chomped down on it.

The room was quiet by the time Charlotte remembered they had an audience. Ainsley and Maisy were both staring at them curiously. Alex arched an eyebrow at her brother as she bit back a smirk. Meemaw donned a self-satisfied grin.

Charlotte abruptly pulled her leg from his grip, her body instantly missing the warmth of his palm. She dropped her gaze to her plate, attacking what remained of her chicken salad with gusto.

"Behave," Val scolded her son.

It didn't go unnoticed by Charlotte that Val took the opportunity to touch Noah every chance she could get. A tender brush of her hand along his back as she passed behind his chair when she was refilling the bowl of potato chips. A caress of his biceps when she reached past him to hand Ainsley her sippy cup. Now, she tousled his hair as she stood and cleared the plates.

It must have been difficult for Val during those long years when Alex was sick, devoting most of her time and energy to her ailing daughter. Charlotte couldn't imagine having to choose between Vivi and Gray. Her stomach rolled at the thought. Noah's mother was clearly making up for lost time with her son.

Charlotte wondered if he even noticed. Noah was so good at diverting attention away from himself. It astounded Charlotte that he believed he didn't deserve it. Even when he was outperforming most every other quarterback in the game. Case in point: tonight's honor.

Her heart ached for the man sitting beside her, who was still holding on to the traits of his childhood. Still denying himself the spotlight he deserved. She wanted to rest her hand on his thigh in comfort. If only she trusted herself.

"I'm sure your father would like it if you stopped by the high school this afternoon," Meemaw said as she tossed her keys across the kitchen table to him. "The boys would love a pep talk before tonight's game. Before you hurry off, fetch Charlotte's bag, and bring it over to my place."

"Your place?"

"Noah, she is not sleeping on your top bunk," Val said.

"Charlotte can have my old room. But that means the girls will have to sleep with you, baby brother." Alex's offer didn't really sound like a legitimate one.

"Nonsense." Meemaw strode toward the door leading to the breezeway that adjoined the two houses. "I told everyone a real live princess will be sleeping at my house. And that's what is happening."

"Meemaw, Charlotte isn't—" Noah started to say.

Charlotte shushed him. "It's your grandmother's birthday. If she wants me to be a princess, then I'm a princess." She turned and curtsied to Meemaw. "Which makes you the queen." Maisy and Ainsley giggled. Charlotte mimed tapping them both on the head with a wand. "And you are both ladies-in-waiting."

Maisy grabbed hold of Charlotte's hand while Ainsley curled her sticky fingers around one of Charlotte's.

"Come on." Maisy tugged them toward the breezeway. "Meemaw's guest bed is really bouncy."

"It's a big bed, too. Plenty of room for both of you. And I take my hearing aids out at night, so whatever you get up to, I won't hear a thing." Meemaw said with a wink.

"Christ," Noah moaned behind them.

TWELVE

"IS SHE HERE WITH YOU?" The receptionist practically squealed the question at Noah when he stepped into the front office of the high school.

"Well, hello to you, too, Mrs. Weaver. And no, my sister isn't here with me. She stayed at home with the girls." He knew damn well Elisa Weaver wasn't asking about Alex. "Is my dad in his office?"

She rolled her eyes before gesturing with her chin in the direction of the assistant principal's office. Scott Hudson served triple duty at the small high school as its football coach, athletic director, and assistant principal. His brown eyes lit up when he spied his son in the doorway. He waved Noah into his office.

"I'm glad he was able to get his grades up, too, Mrs. Thompkins," his dad said into his cellphone. "We need him on the field tonight." He made the "hurry up" gesture with his hand as Mrs. Thompkins continued to gush at the good news. "Yes, of course. Great. Yes. We'll see you tonight then. Goodbye."

Noah's dad blew out a sigh of relief after ending the call.

"You made her day," Noah said.

"And you just made my day." His father gave Noah a side hug, complete with two hard pats on the back. "Hell of a game last night. On both sides of the ball. I'm proud of you, son. Always have been."

"Thanks. It was a team effort."

His dad made a sound at the back of his throat. "Yes, it was. But you are the leader of one half of that team when it's on the field. It's okay to take a little credit for yourself occasionally."

"From the looks of it, I don't have a choice today."

"Okay, yeah." His dad put his hands up. "That's on me. The boosters wanted to do it last year as a way to draw some attention—and outside funding—to the school's athletic programs. I knew you were busy trying to find your place in the league and you'd hate any sort of additional recognition, so I stalled them. Once you were named player of the week at the start of this season, though, there was no holding them back."

"You might have mentioned it to me."

"Have you met your grandmother? She was the one leading the charge with the boosters. She insisted you wouldn't show up if we told you." He eyed Noah. "Given your reaction, I agree with her."

Noah dropped into one of the two chairs in front of his father's desk. "The media have been a bitch. You know that. I'd prefer to stay away from the glare of the spotlight when I can."

His father stared down at him for a long moment before walking over to close his office door. He sat down in the chair opposite Noah.

"It was a small-town story until you brought your—" He made air quotes. "—Friend, the princess, with you."

Noah let out a groan as he tilted his head back. "Not you, too, Dad. You do know she's not a princess, right?"

"I realize that. But what I'm trying to determine is how good of a friend is she?"

Let me know when you figure it out, Noah wanted to say.

He met his father's questioning gaze. The man's brown eyes, a mirror image of his own, always compelled Noah to tell the truth. Their build was so similar that both of his nieces had mistaken Noah for their Gramps on more than one occasion. The only striking difference was their hair. His dad was prematurely gray. The stress of Alex's cancer battle had seen to that.

"I don't know," Noah admitted before he could rein in the words. "I mean, yeah, we're friends."

They were, weren't they?

"That's not the impression I get when I see photos of you two."

Do you always kiss your friends like you're the last two people on Earth?

Noah sat forward in the chair, draping his clasped hands between his knees. "Honestly, dad, I don't know what we are." He hung his head.

"What do you want to be?"

Everything. "It doesn't matter. She leads a very different life than I do."

"Does she? Maybe she grew up differently—"

Noah hiked up his eyebrows.

"Okay, very differently. But at the end of the day, when it's just the two of you, are you actually that different?"

"I do know that she's not the person the media makes her out to be. Not anymore, anyway. And she was a kid back then. Trying to find herself."

"There you go." His father tapped him on the knee.

"But is that enough, Dad?"

His father shrugged. "Hard to say. Life, love, marriage, they don't come with a playbook. Where would the fun be in that?"

"Failure isn't fun."

"No, but you've never shied away from going for something when the results weren't guaranteed."

"Not the same. Football is a game. Love isn't."

"Ah ha." His father grinned behind his steepled fingers. "You do love her, then."

Christ, did he ever. He let out a long-suffering groan as he dragged his fingers through his hair.

"Is that such a bad thing?" his dad asked. "And don't give me any more of that crap about you being from different worlds. You both bring a certain amount of notoriety to the relationship. And it doesn't matter how you grew up. How you go forward is what's important."

"Relationships are hard enough without your every move being dissected on social media."

His father chuckled as he stood. "There's no requirement that she be at the game tonight."

"I told her that. She wants to come anyway."

"Then that should tell you all you need to know, son." His father dropped his hand to Noah's shoulder and gave it a gentle squeeze. "Come on. The team will suit up for practice soon. I'm sure they'd love a couple of pointers."

He stood to follow his dad. "Do you think Meemaw might have faked her illness last night to guilt me into bringing Charlotte?"

His father's eyes widened before he bellowed out a laugh. "You know something? I wouldn't put it past her."

A MUFFLED groan coming from the other side of the house had Charlotte dashing from the guest room.

"Meemaw? Are you okay?"

Please don't let anything happen to Noah's grandmother. It will wreck him.

"In here."

Charlotte breathed a little easier as she hurried through the elegant bedroom, ignoring the heirloom antiques it was decorated with. She slid to a halt in the adjoining bathroom. Meemaw was seated in front of an ornate makeup mirror, wiping her eyes.

"What happened?" Charlotte sank down on her heels beside the upholstered bench Meemaw was perched on.

"Life happened." The older woman waved a brow pencil. "The years stole my eyebrows. Old age makes my hands shake so that now I can't even draw new ones on."

"Is that all?"

"Says the perky twenty-something. Just you wait, young lady." Meemaw pinned her with her most haughty look.

She couldn't help it. Charlotte laughed as she took the eyebrow pencil from the older woman's hand.

"Here. Let me help."

"Oh, don't mind me. You scoot. I heard you on the phone with your office. You're too busy running a beauty empire to waste time on an old gal like me."

"Nonsense. I would be a fool to resist the chance to glam up a sophisticated, seasoned woman." Charlotte knee-walked in front of Meemaw. "It's market research."

"Oooo, I like that. I'm not old. I'm seasoned." She lifted her chin to study her face in the mirror while Charlotte sorted through the makeup on the counter.

"It's been a while since I've done someone else's makeup.

This will be fun." She slipped a headband on Meemaw to keep her hair back.

"I would think running a company would be much more exciting. Not to mention fulfilling."

"Mmm." Charlotte tested out the various colors of pencils on her hand before holding it up to Meemaw's face. "It was."

"Was? You don't enjoy running Truly You? How come?"

Charlotte traced the brow pencil along the bottom arch of Meemaw's sparse eyebrows. "I love Truly like it was my child. But like most kids, it's growing up. And outgrowing me."

This was the first time she could speak the words without that stabbing pain of not being good enough. Noah was right. She'd been skilled enough to get the company off the ground. To get it where it was today before handing it off to investors. That was how most companies worked. Instead of feeling like a failure, she needed to revel in her success.

"Hmm," the older woman said. "Perhaps it's time to get yourself some actual children."

A lump formed in Charlotte's throat. A child of her own had been a dream since she was barely out of her teens.

"You're not subtle at all."

"At my age, I don't have that kind of luxury."

Charlotte admired her handiwork with the brow pencil before reaching for some eye shadow. "I'm having a hard time finding a man who wants to take me on."

She didn't have to elaborate further. Meemaw's humph sounded as frustrated as Charlotte felt.

"He's a lot like his grandfather."

"How so?"

Meemaw's smile was a wistful one. "Ross didn't want me to be tied down to a Navy pilot who would be off on a ship for six months at a time. He thought I deserved a man who'd be around to treat me like a queen every day." She chuckled.

"My daddy owned the furniture company that employed most of the people in these parts. Everyone thought we were next to royalty."

She arched an eyebrow at Charlotte before she continued.

"Ross didn't think he measured up financially, either. And neither did he want to be stuck in western North Carolina running someone else's dream once my daddy died. He was going to be an airline pilot. He wouldn't be rich. But he would be happy."

Was that what was holding Noah back? Some neanderthal hang-up on the difference in their socioeconomic status? Charlotte almost laughed. Guess he possessed an ego after all.

What he didn't realize was her money hadn't come from working hard and employing a talent like his did. Noah's wealth was worth so much more. And if she took away her trust fund and compared the measly salary that she paid herself from Truly next to the one he earned playing football, then he was the clear breadwinner.

Men are so stupid.

"Obviously he came around," Charlotte said.

"You betcha he did." She spread out her arms. "I'm irresistible."

Both women laughed before Meemaw sobered up.

"Men need a little help connecting the dots sometimes. Once I spelled it out for him, letting him know in no uncertain terms that the only thing I needed in life was him, he came around."

Charlotte stroked some blush on Meemaw's cheeks as she contemplated the older woman's words.

Could it be that easy?

Noah's grandmother placed two fingers beneath Charlotte's chin and lifted it until their eyes met. "Mark my words, that boy is in love with you. It's obvious to anyone who sees the way he looks at you. Sure, I might have used underhanded tactics to get Noah to bring you home with him. But, know this, Charlotte Davis, if he didn't want you here, he would have ignored me."

She fingered the three silver affirmation bracelets on Charlotte's wrist.

"Faith. Hope. Love." She recited the single word inscribed on each one. "'The greatest of these is love.' Millions of women buy these from your company and wear them hoping to manifest these thoughts into reality. You should take a page from your own book and do the same."

"DUDE I MUST LOVE your sister if I'm wearing your jersey and not mine," Noah's brother-in-law, Chris, remarked when he wandered up beside Noah at the pregame tailgate in the high school parking lot a few hours later. Alex's high school sweetheart had played defensive back for Noah's dad while Noah was still in elementary school. Suffice it to say, Chris was Noah's first real football idol. He even threatened to run away from home when Alex and Chris broke up briefly.

Chris gave him a little shoulder check. "This is kind of crazy, huh? Although it's probably second nature to you, seeing strangers decked out in your digits."

Noah had to agree that it was still a little bizarre. Especially since so many people were wearing jerseys sporting his high school number, eleven years after he last took the field as the school's quarterback. Maisy and Ainsley danced around in tricked-out versions his mother made for them, twirling their pom-poms with wild exuberance. A few folks milling around were even wearing a replica of his college jersey.

Not that Noah noticed any longer. The singular focus of his attention was on the gorgeous woman who had just rolled up with his mother and Meemaw. Charlotte looked like she'd just walked out of his high school fantasies, wearing his letterman jacket over a silk turtleneck. She'd paired it with the skin hugging jeans and boots she'd left home with this morning. An excited murmur rose from the crowd as the three women made their way over to Noah and his family.

"I hope you don't mind." She looked almost shy as she gestured to the jacket.

Mind? Nope, he didn't mind at all. He liked the idea of her wearing something of his. Of her announcing to the world that she belonged to him. A vivid image of her wearing his jersey and nothing else swam before his eyes. Without thinking, he reached for the sides of the jacket and tugged it tighter around her. The move had the happy coincidence of bringing them closer together.

"Nah, I outgrew it years ago." He lowered his voice. "It looks better on you than it ever did on me, anyway."

The corners of her lips twitched at the compliment.

"I'll second that," Chris interjected from beside them.

Noah shot his brother-in-law a look he'd seen Devlin employ to send defensive linemen scurrying. It worked like a charm.

"You know, I think I hear Ainsley crying," Chris mumbled before he disappeared into the crowd.

He'd no sooner left, however, when the president of the boosters stepped in.

"Are you ready for your big entrance, Noah?" he asked.

Noah bit back a groan. The boosters expected him to flex the entire night, beginning with a stadium entrance riding in the back of a convertible with the marching band accompanying him. All this showboating was ridiculous.

"Your family is headed into the stadium. I should go with them," Charlotte said quietly.

And the last thing he wanted to do was let Charlotte out of his sight.

Maybe not ever.

Noah looked over at her. How could he have ever believed they were from two different worlds? Out of his reach? He knew the real woman behind the moniker. He'd known her since that night in London. And she was looking at him with the same cautious optimism gripping his gut.

How you go forward is what's important.

His father's words echoed in his head. He reached for her hand to keep her from walking away. "Go for a ride with me."

It was only after the words were out of his mouth that Noah realized his question wasn't literal. There was so much more he wanted from this incredible woman. The ride into the stadium was symbolic of the beginning of a lot more. At least he hoped so. A sweat broke out at the back of his neck when Charlotte blinked several times before slaying him with a guileless smile, so beautiful it damn near knocked the wind out of him.

"I would be honored," she whispered as she laced her fingers through his and curled into his shoulder.

He lifted their joined hands and kissed her fingers. "Let's give 'em something to talk about."

She threw back her head and laughed.

THIRTEEN

CHARLOTTE HAD a hard time concentrating on the action on the field. Especially with Noah looking ruggedly handsome in his rollneck sweater and well-worn jeans. From the moment he took her hand earlier, he hadn't let go. Throughout the game, he sat with his solid body pressed up against hers so that they were joined from knee to shoulder. She resented every time the team scored because it meant having to stand from their deliciously warm cocoon and cheer.

Then there was the funnel cake. A delicacy unfamiliar to Charlotte, but something she was going to enjoy again and again. Especially if it meant Noah would nibble at the trace of powdered sugar on the corner of her lip. Sophie wasn't going to let her live it down when that particular image landed on social media.

Her friend was probably crowing over video likely already posted of Charlotte at mid-field planting a congratulatory kiss on Noah's lips after the dedication was complete. It was a bold move, she knew, but she was taking Meemaw's words to heart. Going for what she wanted.

Something had shifted between them tonight. Noah was no longer acting like the man who'd once vowed she wasn't his type. Rather, he seemed proud and almost grateful to have her by his side as he navigated the evening. Both feelings she was experiencing herself.

And there was no mistaking the hunger in his eyes, either. Each time his gaze landed on her, the longing she saw reflected there stirred up the pent-up need he'd left her with last night. And every other time he'd touched her. She was grateful when the game ended with a win for the home team.

Forty-five minutes later, they were still trying to work their way past the well-wishers and fans who wanted to glad-hand with Noah. Charlotte tried to hang back, letting him have his moment, but Noah wasn't having it, keeping her glued to his side. He appeared to no longer care about dodging the media, pulling her into selfies with fans. She tried not to think about the feeding frenzy Bucky Kincaid was going to have with all the videos from the evening. That was a worry for another day.

The parking lot had cleared out when they reached Meemaw's truck.

"Looks like the rest of your family left us." She leaned her back against the driver's door.

"Mmm," was all he said.

Noah braced his hands on the roof of the cab, caging her in. Not that she felt trapped. Rather, she felt protected.

And desired.

"Is this the part of the evening where you lure me behind the bleachers?" she teased.

Noah scoffed. "Not private enough."

His hips bumped against hers when he moved in closer. Charlotte smothered a gasp at the contact. She pressed her palms to his chest, trailing her fingers along the soft waffle stitching of his cotton sweater.

"I have a confession to make," she told him. "I wasn't exactly honest with you last night."

Another scoff. "Do tell."

"I did come to last night's game with the express purpose of cheering for you." She dropped her voice to a whisper. "And hopefully seeing you."

He looked like he'd stopped breathing. The streetlight behind his head made his face unreadable.

Charlotte forged on. "I came back to Baltimore because —" A shaky sigh escaped. "Because no matter what I do, I can't stop thinking about you."

Noah went still as a statue. She could feel his warm breath whispering against her cheek. Her fingers slid along the stubble of his jaw before they traced his bottom lip.

"And if I have to beg you to kiss me, I will."

He jerked away from her. Charlotte immediately mourned the loss of his body heat. And very probably her dignity.

"Noah?" she croaked.

He fumbled with his jeans pocket until the locks on the truck chirped.

"Get in the truck, Charlotte."

Seriously? Was he rejecting her again? She shook her head.

"I don't understand."

He reached behind her to open the door, the streetlight illuminating his face. His expression was strained. When she touched his forearm, his nostrils flared.

"Woman, get in the truck so I can take you home and do things to you that I'd rather do in private," he bit out through clenched teeth. "Please."

"Oh. *Ohhhh!*"

As soon as he yanked the door open, she scooted across the seat. He followed, turning the ignition and jerking the truck into motion. The five-minute ride felt like an eternity. If Charlotte had been restless sitting beside Noah on the bleachers and not being able to act on her desire, she was practically burning up with lust now. She started to shrug out of his jacket.

"Don't." His rough comment had her pulling up short. He steered the truck into the driveway. "I've been dreaming about undressing you for three fucking years. Don't you dare deprive me of that fantasy now."

Oh. My.

She froze with her arm halfway out of one sleeve as the truck lurched to a halt. Noah was out of the cab and around to the passenger side before she could right herself. He reached out a hand, but then seemed to think better of it.

"If I touch you now, we won't make it inside."

His coarsely uttered words had her panties wet. One by one, the motion-sensor lights blinked on as she marched swiftly toward Meemaw's front door. He reached around her to punch in the code on the lock. They were welcomed by a single lamp illuminating the foyer, coupled with the sound of his grandmother's soft snores drifting in from the back bedroom.

Charlotte experienced a brief lick of apprehension. "She wasn't kidding about taking out her hearing aids, was she?" she whispered.

Noah groaned. "You're killing me, Princess."

He jerked his chin toward the guest bedroom. Her pulse kicked up another notch at his assertiveness. Noah was a man of action. There would be no false platitudes or rambling soliloquies about his desire for her when they reached the bedroom. Based on their earlier encounters, his mouth and his hands would do all the talking.

The very thought was already driving her wild. Sinking her teeth into her bottom lip, she began sauntering backwards. He followed, his focus intent on her mouth.

One of the bedside lamps was left on, casting a seductive glow over the queen-sized bed. Backing into the room, Charlotte could feel her annoying self-doubt start to rear its ugly head. What if she messed this up again? This wasn't like a casual fling with one of the banal trust fund boys of her past. This was Noah prowling toward her.

A man of substance.

The man she'd been longing for since before she even knew he existed. There was something about him that felt so true. So perfect. It was as if he was the missing piece that she'd been longing for her entire life. She'd known that rightness the moment she woke up beside him that long ago morning in London.

And, just like that, she knew she wouldn't mess this up. Because this was Noah. The only person she could be herself around. The only person who gave the impression of liking her for herself. Not her trust fund.

He closed the door and Charlotte's knees quivered slightly. She drew in a deep breath, squaring her shoulders and jutting her chin up. A sly smile formed on his lips as he closed the distance between them.

A low, almost-feral sound escaped his mouth when he stopped mere inches from her.

"You have no idea how many nights I've dreamt of this," he said before lifting one hand to delicately finger the collar of his jacket she was wearing.

She canted her head so she could lean her cheek against his wandering fingers. "Actually, I have a pretty good idea."

He smiled at that, this grin relaxed and perhaps a little awestruck. His fingers moved to feather over her cheek. "I need to know this is what you want."

Of course he would ask that now. Most guys waited until both parties were hot and bothered before asking for acquiescence. Not that Charlotte wasn't already bordering on combustible. Still, she appreciated that Noah's character ran deep.

She rested her palms against his abdomen, letting a finger slide beneath his sweater. He flinched when she traced along the taut skin just above the waistband of his jeans. "I want this," she whispered. "With you."

The last word was barely out of her mouth before he kissed her. Only this kiss was unlike any he'd given her before. The hunger was still there, sure. Yet this kiss was different.

More reverent.

More tender.

More devoted.

Charlotte swallowed a sob of joy as she kissed him back, eager to convey the same emotions. It didn't take long for things to heat up, though. They'd started down this road a time or two before, and their mouths were becoming attuned to each other.

Tongues tangled as their hands wandered. Her hips swayed into his. A moan escaped the back of her throat when she brushed up against his hard length.

He tugged the jacket down her shoulders. She moaned again, more plaintive this time, when she was forced to remove her hands from his body so she could shrug out of the jacket. Noah had the nerve to chuckle against her mouth. It turned into a groan when her palm found the bulge in his jeans.

Noah nipped at her lip in response before soothing it with

his tongue. His hands skimmed along the arms of her turtle-neck, moving up and over the silk until his thumbs were torturing her nipples at the same time as he ravaged her mouth. When she began to fumble with the button on his fly, he dropped his hands to her waist, gripping her firmly so he could put some space between their bodies. Charlotte let out a tiny cry of frustration.

He dropped his chin to his chest. "We've got all night," he mumbled, sounding as if he was giving himself a little pep talk.

"Yes, we do. I'm not going anywhere."

Her whispered reassurance was all the encouragement he needed. He yanked the hem of her shirt up her torso. Her arms and hair got tangled in the silk. Noah wasted no time taking advantage of her captivity, bowing his head, and scraping his teeth over her nipple, already straining through the satin fabric of her bra. Charlotte swore, frantically working her arms free, then pulling the fabric from her hair.

Their eyes locked. The hunger she saw in his expression took her breath away. It also had her feeling a tad self-conscious. She reached up to tame her wild hair.

"Don't." He brushed her hands away before working his fingers through what had to be a riotous mess.

"I'm sure I look like a troll," she mumbled.

He chuckled. "Your hair is exactly like you. Wild." He tugged her closer. "Unpredictable." His tongue teased one corner of her mouth. "Exciting."

She tried to capture his lips with hers, but he was having none of it. Instead, exploring the tender skin beneath her ear.

"Unique." He nibbled along her collarbone.

Her knees did that wobbly thing again, while the rest of her grew taut with longing. She dug her nails into his shoulders.

"And unbelievably gorgeous," he whispered before giving her what she wanted.

He ravished her mouth at the same time as he edged their bodies closer to the bed. Seconds later, they toppled onto the mattress, their mouths still fused, their arms and legs tangled together. He rolled her beneath him, aligning his body between her legs. She gasped into the kiss at the feel of him rubbing against her aching core.

"On second thought," she panted once she managed to coax her mouth from his. "I'm not willing to wait all night. I need you naked. Now."

His arched eyebrow told her she'd likely pay for her bossiness later. To her relief, he pushed up onto his forearms, reached behind his head with one hand and tugged the sweater off. He sent it sailing into the shadows.

"Finally," she moaned, letting her fingers slide along the smooth muscles of his competitor's body. Feeling the heat of his gaze, she tore her attention away from her mission to map out his shape, lifting her arms so he could free her from her bra. Her boots hit the floor with two loud thumps, followed by his sneakers.

Before she knew it, they were both naked, skin-to-skin, on the bed. Noah hummed with appreciation, while his lips undertook a slow, torturous exploration of her body.

"Noah," she moaned when her nerve endings were so aroused, she didn't think she could take it any longer. She was growing frantic to have him inside her.

But this was Noah. Of course, he was going to take care of her first. And, as it turns out, Noah was a talker during sex. The consummate gentleman, asking for permission before every move.

Is it okay if I touch you here?

Do you like it this way?

May I kiss you here?

Is it good for you?

Yes, yes, yes! She cried, writhing beneath him. He placated her with not one, but two toe-curling orgasms.

She wanted to do the same for him. Touching him everywhere she could reach. Learning how to make him moan with pleasure, too. And when he looked at her one last time, a silent request for permission in his eyes, the foil packet in his fingers, Charlotte whipped it away from him and tore it open.

"Yes, Noah. Please, God, yes."

He eased into her, swallowing her gasp of pleasure with a kiss. Their bodies lined up perfectly, like two halves of the same piece. He propped himself up on his elbows, staring down at her with a half-drunk smile on his face. She hiked up her hips to allow him to seat himself deeper.

"Mmm." He stared down at her, his expression pure male satisfaction, appearing to savor the moment.

Clenching her muscles around him, she reached up and brushed that untamed piece of hair out of his eyes.

"Don't you dare ask me permission one more time," she told him. "I want this. So, so much."

That's all it took for him to shed his polite demeanor and show off his athletic prowess. He moved like a man possessed with want.

"Yes," she murmured in encouragement.

His breathing became more fractured with every stroke. Charlotte cried out with delight, wrapping her legs more securely around his hips. He muttered something lethal sounding when she began scoring her nails along his back. Their bodies, now slick with exertion, were moving in perfect synchronicity. Her hips kept pace with him thrust for thrust until the humming in her veins threatened to overwhelm her.

"Noah," she begged. "Please."

She thought he might have chuckled at her plea. But then he sent her flying over the edge and all she could think about was the unadulterated bliss ebbing through her body. With a very un-Noah-like savage groan, he thrust into her one last time, then collapsed beside her.

FOURTEEN

NOAH FINGERED the silky strands of Charlotte's hair where they fanned out over his chest. Her sigh of contentment whispered over his skin. He snuggled her in closer against him, reveling in the feel of her naked body. His junk grew unapologetically tight when he inhaled the familiar scent of her skin, now mingled with the musky smell of sex.

Christ.

He'd just had the best sex of his life and his body was already begging for another round. Not that he could blame himself. He seriously doubted he'd ever grow tired of having this woman.

Of hearing his name on her lips when she came.

Of feeling her velvety muscles clenching around him, urging him on to a mind-blowing release.

Of feeling her heart beating against his.

This is what it feels like to be complete.

Funny how Noah never knew what he was missing before this vibrant, impulsive, larger-than-life woman exploded into his life. He'd wrongly believed all he needed was success on the football field—and his family—to be fulfilled. Clearly, he was an idiot.

He brushed a kiss along the top of her head. "Thank you."

Thank you for opening my eyes. For being you. For giving yourself to me.

"Mmm," she murmured against his shoulder. "I think you're the first guy to ever thank me for sex."

"Get used to it," he growled while trying to ignore the ugly sensation churning deep in his gut at the thought of anyone else experiencing what he just had with Charlotte.

Wearing a smug smile, she rolled onto his chest, letting her long legs drop to either side of his hips. His breath hitched when she settled her core on the part of him arguing for an immediate repeat performance. Charlotte was noticeably less affected, her focus intent on tracing a finger along his shoulder.

"I owe you a thank you, too. Thank you for having my back that night in London. You could have walked away." She looked up at him then, her blue eyes melancholy. "You probably should have walked away given all the bad karma that came about because you played along with me."

As if.

There was no way he could deny Charlotte anything she asked of him, even back then. Besides, he'd never walk away from a woman in need of rescuing. Even knowing the bullshit Bucky Kincaid would heap on him, Noah would still make the same decision.

He brushed a piece of hair back from her face. "You're worth it."

She looked away. "You say that now. You didn't think so once upon a time."

Noah slammed his eyes shut with a groan. "The things

you overheard. I didn't mean them. My ego took a serious blow, and I acted like an ass."

There was a ghost of a smile on her lips when he opened his eyes. She traced a circle on his chest. He rested his palm on her cheek.

"I'm sorry I hurt you," he said solemnly. It pained him to know she'd felt less than because of the idiotic things he had spoken out of spite.

"I guess we both did some stupid things. Something tells me we still have some issues, though. Mainly the big one about you thinking you're not good enough for me."

He jerked his eyes to the ceiling, swearing violently under his breath. "Meemaw has a big mouth."

"She's not afraid to speak her mind. To tell it like it is. I adore that about her."

Noah almost laughed. He was right about the two women being alike. There should probably be an emergency alert broadcast every time those two got together.

"And for your information, I'm working hard not to be hoity-toity and snobbish anymore."

The sight of her bottom lip quivering sent a stab of pain to his chest. He reversed their positions. She let out a little shriek that he silenced with his lips.

"It was never about you," he said when she was pliant beneath him. "It's more about my hang-ups. I'm a small-town boy who hasn't seen much of the world. I don't want you to wake up one day and decide I'm not enough."

There. He'd said it out loud. She opened her mouth to protest, but he silenced her with another kiss.

"You're going to tell me it doesn't matter," he murmured against her mouth. "And in my head, I know that. But it's very much a guy thing. I want to be your everything."

Her eyes were shining with unshed tears when she shoved at his chest. He pushed up to balance on his forearms.

"You stupid, stupid, man." She sniffed. "I don't want a jet-setting playboy. I want a man who will kiss me senseless in an elevator then lay beside me on a hotel bed and watch my favorite movie without getting all handsy. The perfect guy for me is the one who crouches down to meet a sick little boy in the eye. A man who allows his wily grandmother to con him into bringing a girl home for her birthday." She cradled his chin with her fingers. "Don't you see, Noah? This small town is the place where you get the most attractive part of you. Your integrity. I don't want a guy who can order a martini in five different languages. I want a guy whose entire town admires him so much they'll show up at a high school football game wearing his jersey."

"You make it sound a lot more glamorous than it is."

She shook her head in exasperation. "You don't realize how lucky you are to have grown up in a place where you have connections and history. I was raised in Manhattan among a million other people who only made it a point to know me because of what I might be able to offer them—money."

He leaned down to touch his forehead to hers. Anyone who'd stood in a grocery store checkout line for the past twenty years had—thanks to the tabloids—a front-row seat as Charlotte went from poor-little-rich-girl to princess. Sure, Noah's life growing up hadn't been easy, given what his family had to endure. But there was a lot of truth to what she said. Like it or not, this town had given him a safety net to live his life as he wanted.

"You'll always be more than enough for me, Noah Hudson," she whispered. "You were exactly what I needed and wanted from the moment we met."

He swallowed roughly. She was wrong. He was so unworthy of this woman. Except he wasn't going to deny himself any longer. She wanted him. She believed in him. He'd do whatever it took to make himself the man she thought him to be. Beginning right now, by making her shout his name in ecstasy again.

———

NOAH'S DAD nudged him with his shoulder. "You look a lot more relaxed than you did when you arrived yesterday."

"Mmm," he replied, keeping his focus aimed at the women in his life who were dancing with one another in the middle of the VFW hall. Maisy spun around the dance floor like a whirling dervish. Ainsley chortled as she swayed side to side with her feet balanced on Noah's mom's shoes, while Alex and Charlotte tried to teach Meemaw the latest line dance.

Charlotte didn't need a ball gown to look like a princess. Even dressed in a simple black jersey dress, she enchanted everyone around her. Meemaw guffawed when Charlotte twirled her around. How had he ever doubted she would fit in?

"She acts very down-to-earth." His father nodded in Charlotte's direction. "Not that I've gotten to exchange more than two words with her. You two must have made a day of it, exploring the area."

Noah tucked his chin so his dad wouldn't see the telltale blush warming his cheeks. They had made a day of it. Exploring each other, as well as the surrounding mountains and waterfalls. He'd had the best intentions when they started out this morning. It was Charlotte's fault for disarming his plans when she'd teased him about taking her to all the area make-out spots. It would have been a shame to disappoint her.

His father patted him on the shoulder. "I'm glad you've found something besides football to focus on. I don't remember ever seeing you looking this happy."

"You sound like Meemaw." His grandmother had been smugly basking in the fruits of her manipulation all weekend.

His father chuckled. "Today I'll take that as a compliment. And while you stand here admiring the view, I'm going to take this young lady of yours for a spin around the dance floor."

"I was just about to do that," Noah grumbled.

"You snooze, you lose," his dad called over his shoulder while making a beeline for Charlotte. "It's your grandmother's birthday. Dance with her."

His father's words had Meemaw arching an eyebrow expectantly at Noah. Charlotte's blue eyes sparkled with delight when his father began circling her around the dance floor to the tune of a Bobby Darin ballad. With no graceful way of getting out of it, Noah held out his hands to his grandmother.

"I'll take my thank you sooner rather than later," she said once they began dancing. "I'm not getting any younger, you know."

"Gloat much."

She had the nerve to laugh. "Admit it. I was right. You followed my advice and brought Charlotte. She showed her true colors, just like I said she would."

The woman in question was chatting animatedly with his father, as though the two were long-lost friends. Noah couldn't keep the smile from his lips. She had shown her true colors. He'd guessed she was nothing like the spoiled woman the headlines made her out to be. And he was glad his family got to see the low-maintenance, unassuming side of her, too.

"The girls from the garden club were all clutching their pearls when Charlotte began clearing the empty paper plates and cups into the trash." Meemaw donned a proud smile, as if Charlotte had just won an Olympic gold medal or something. "She's good people. And she's good for you."

"Mmm."

Meemaw smacked him on the shoulder. "Don't you dare spoil it by doubting yourself. You're good for her, too. She needs someone like you to center her. That poor girl has been chasing after normalcy all her life. You can give her that."

"Wow, Meemaw, is that your way of saying I'm boring?"

His grandmother glared at him. "More like impossible. You are going to mess this up, aren't you?"

He pulled her in for a hug just as the song ended. "I won't mess it up, Meemaw. I promise. Happy birthday." He pressed a kiss to her forehead.

"I told you to dance with her. Not make her cry," his father said when he and Charlotte made their way over to them.

"Oh hush, you." Meemaw dabbed at her eyes. "These are happy tears. Now, are you going to dance with your mother tonight, or what?"

Noah's dad shot him a long-suffering look before steering his mother in the other direction. "At Last," by Etta James wafted from the speakers. Charlotte smiled as she stepped into Noah's arms.

"Appropriate," she murmured, snaking her arms over his shoulders.

"Mmm." He leaned his forehead against hers and they began to sway in place to the music. "Have I thanked you yet for coming with me this weekend?"

"Let's see. I recall several times when you thanked me last night. And again, today at the falls, followed by a spectacular reenactment in the shower once we got home." She inched her hips closer. "But if you're still feeling grateful, I'll let you thank me again tonight."

He let out a tortured groan before burying his face against her neck.

Charlotte had the nerve to laugh at his discomfort. He was just about to drag her into the utility room at the back of the hall where he could thank her properly, when two hands wrapped themselves tightly around his legs.

"Uncle Noah. Mommy says you're not doing it right."

Maisy smiled up at him with the certainty of a four-year-old who would likely rule the world one day given the genes flowing through her veins. His sister shot him a saucy grin from across the dance floor. Chris shrugged his shoulders, already whipped by the women in his household. Not to be denied, Ainsley toddled over, punch drunk with exhaustion. Waving her arms up to Charlotte, she unleashed a pitiful wail.

"Oh, sweetie, come here." Charlotte lifted his niece into her arms.

Ainsley shot her sister a satisfied smirk before resting her head on Charlotte's shoulder.

"Hey! I want to dance with you guys, too."

He was already hefting Maisy onto his hip before she could finish her demand. Maisy wrapped an arm around Charlotte's and Noah's necks, pulling the foursome closer together.

"This is perfect," Maisy announced.

It certainly is.

Charlotte gently rocked Ainsley. The little girl's eyes drifted shut.

"Do you want me to take her, too," he asked when she shifted Ainsley on her shoulder.

She shook her head. "I miss when Vivi and Gray were this small. I used to dance them to sleep just like this."

The gentle smile she bestowed on his niece robbed him of his breath. Her devotion to her brother's twins was touching. It was obvious Charlotte longed for children of her own. He could give her that. Hell, he ached to give her that.

A round of applause greeted them when the music stopped. It was only then that he noticed all eyes in the room focused their way. Charlotte curtsied as best she could with twenty-five pounds of dead weight on her shoulder. Maisy trotted out her best royal wave for the crowd.

Alex and Chris hurried over to take their daughters. Noah reached for Charlotte's hand, brushing his lips over her fingers. A gorgeous blush stained her cheeks when she leaned her cheek against his shoulder. Noah was a little disappointed there wasn't a camera in sight to record the moment. For once, he'd like to give Bucky Kincaid something to eat crow about.

"Is it time to go home?" Charlotte whispered, the seductively asked question erasing all thoughts of Kincaid from his mind.

FIFTEEN

THE SKY WAS a brilliant blue when Charlotte and Noah emerged from Meemaw's the following morning. Stopping on the breezeway connecting the two houses, Charlotte inhaled a deep breath of the mountain air, tinged with the crisp scent of autumn.

"It's so beautiful," she said.

Noah wrapped his arms around her from behind, burying his lips into her hair. "Mmm. You are."

She swatted at his hands that were roaming shamelessly over her belly. "I meant this place. Your home. I'm so glad you invited me."

"We could go back inside where you can thank me for my generous hospitality."

The idea was appealing, but if he "thanked" her anymore today, she doubted she'd be able to walk.

"We're late for breakfast," she argued half-heartedly. "Haven't you worked up an appetite yet?"

He spun her around in his arms. The roguish smile he wore was still new to her. And precious. She enjoyed knowing the part of Noah he reserved for only a few. It made her feel special.

And loved.

He hadn't come out and said it yet. At least not in words. But every time he touched her, she experienced it. And it felt glorious.

Her fingers found the buttons on his Henley. "Well, I guess since we're already late." She batted her eyelashes.

Noah's pupils dilated. A moment later, he dropped his arms from around her.

"Too late," he teased as he spun her around and patted her on the butt. "Now I'm thinking about bacon."

Charlotte sputtered in protest. Noah laughed as he propelled her into the empty kitchen.

"There better be bacon left," Noah called out.

"In here," Chris answered.

They found everyone in the family room solemnly staring at the screen of the television mounted on the wall above the fireplace. A fission of unease raced up Charlotte's spine when video of her and Noah at Friday's football game flashed onto the screen.

"And there you have it, irrevocable proof that these two are still a couple. It's always nice to prove you wrong, Bucky," the chirpy blonde who co-anchored the sports network's Sunday pre-game show announced.

The woman's tone had Charlotte wondering if she may have been cornered by Bucky at one point. Bile rose in her throat when the camera cut to Bucky Kincaid's smug grin. Had he always looked so threatening?

"Dude," Chris said. "Did the people in make-up think he was shooting a horror flick?"

Now that she looked closely, Charlotte noticed one of

Bucky's bloodshot eyes had a nervous twitch to it this morning.

"Oh, Hannah," Bucky drawled. "I know how much you love to get the better of me." The bastard winked at the camera. "And I know when to admit I am wrong. It looks like the Blaze QB has, in fact, landed himself a princess."

"Damn straight," Chris yelled at the television.

"Yeah!" Maisy stood and threw a stuffed animal at the screen.

Alex pulled her daughter onto her lap before glaring at her husband over the child's head.

"So, here's my mea culpe, folks," Bucky continued. "Congratulations, bruh. She's all yours."

"What the heck is this guy talking about?" Noah's dad demanded. "What kind of apology is that?"

Bucky wasn't finished. "Just between you and me, though, a word of advice."

"He doesn't need any advice from you," Meemaw barked.

Charlotte had the sudden, eerie feeling she was watching a train wreck. One she was powerless to stop. As much as she wanted to walk away, she couldn't make herself do it.

The camera zoomed in further, accentuating Bucky's manic demeanor. "Keep in mind, Dudson, our princess is fickle."

Noah's hand on her back balled up into a fist at Bucky's use of the word "our."

"Sure, she may choose you now." Bucky's eyes grew more menacing. "But who is to say she won't dump you the way she's dumping her beloved Truly Yours?"

All the heads in the room swiveled to stare at Charlotte. Noah's arm cinched around her waist, pulling her against him protectively.

"The Trulies are all boo-hooing right now." Bucky mimed

rubbing his eyes. "That's right, your princess is selling you out for a quarterback. She's anointing a new CEO and taking her —" Bucky made air quotes with his fingers "—Honest company public."

Charlotte swayed so hard that she might have fallen had she not been leaning against Noah. "That's not true. And he's not supposed to know that."

"Beware, Dudson, or you might find yourself tossed over, too." Bucky held up a photo for the camera. "I'm sure this kid's father didn't enjoy it when it happened to him."

The camera zoomed in on the photo of a very pregnant Charlotte sunbathing at Jay's vineyard in California before the screen went dark.

"You have a baby, Aunt Charlie?" Maisy squeaked.

Alex covered her daughter's mouth with her hand. "It's shameful what they do with AI nowadays."

A painful roaring began in Charlotte's ears. She couldn't seem to get enough air into her lungs. Everyone's perplexed stares made her skin hot and prickly. She pulled away from Noah and bolted out the kitchen door.

Gulping in several deep breaths of fresh air, she race-walked as far away from the house as possible. A wooden swing swayed with the gentle breeze in the distance. It called to her like a beacon in the sea. A picnic table sat beside it. She headed that way, resting her back against the giant oak tree once she reached it. Slamming her eyes shut, she waited for her heart to stop knocking against her chest.

The sound of footsteps on the grass had her lifting her lids. Through the fringe of her lashes, she watched Noah approach. Just like he had that night in London, he wordlessly placed a bottle of water on the picnic table for her. He sat on top of the table, propping his feet on the bench, elbows resting on his knees, the picture of calm as he waited her out.

That was so Noah. He wasn't going to solve this caveman style. He was going to let her have her say. It was one of the things she loved most about him. Her throat constricted painfully, hoping against hope that Bucky hadn't blown it for her.

"That photo isn't fake," she began.

He remained quiet. The only tell that he heard her was the slight clenching of his fingers.

"I was pregnant. It was almost six years ago."

His eyes narrowed for a moment before he made a sound deep in his chest. "The twins. You were their surrogate."

She nodded, too delighted and relieved to form words. God, she loved this brilliant, patient man.

"Come here," he commanded.

Noah lowered himself down onto the bench. She walked over to stand between his knees. Gripping her waist, he pulled her in so that he could press his lips to her stomach. She stroked her fingers through his hair.

"You do know there's no shame in that, right?" he said against the flannel of her shirt.

"I'm not embarrassed. I'm angry. He had no right to tell that story before the twins were old enough to hear it from their parents." She tugged on his hair. "And how dare he make it sound so tawdry."

Noah carefully untangled her fingers from his scalp, moving her hands to his shoulders before he maneuvered his thighs between hers and repositioned her so that she was straddling him on the bench. He brushed a strand of hair from her face. "It's a precious gift you gave them."

Charlotte nodded. "They are precious. I can't imagine my life without them."

He kissed her nose. "They are a part of you."

"I like to think they get their sense of wonder from me."

She sketched a finger along his jawline. "They definitely got their dislike of broccoli from me."

The chuckle rumbling through his chest went a long way toward calming her. Yet, there was still a rather large elephant in the yard with them. Especially since Bucky's words echoed everything Noah feared might happen to their relationship down the road. That she would get bored with him and move on.

"That BS he said about me being flighty. Or fickle. He's wrong, Noah. I meant what I said the other night. You are enough. You'll always be enough."

She kissed him, trying to convey to his senses the words she'd just spoken. Noah had no trouble interpreting her moves. He responded with a delicious kiss of his own.

"The media will not leave us alone," she murmured against his neck. "They will always want to invade our privacy."

He fingered the buttons of her shirt open. "You're worth it." He cupped her breast. "I can't say I like the idea of you walking away from Truly, though. I thought you were going to bring in someone to help. Not sell it."

"I wasn't. I'm not." She huffed. "I'm bringing in a CEO. We're announcing it next week. That's proprietary information, though. Only a handful of people know. I have no idea how Bucky found out." She leaned her forehead on his shoulder. "But maybe I should let it go. It will make things easier. For us."

Noah gave her shoulders a shake. "You are Truly. And Truly is you. I'm not coming between either."

She wasn't sure how to interpret his words.

"You don't have to choose, Charlotte. We're both living extremely privileged lives. We'll make it work. Together."

Tears burned the back of her eyes. "I love you, Noah Hudson. So very much."

He closed his eyes and released a relieved sounding breath. "Good. Because I've been in love with you since that first night in London."

"You have?" she said, not caring about the squeak in her voice.

"I let you win at backgammon, didn't I?"

HER BROTHER SENT his jet to ferry them back to Baltimore. Noah was grateful for the privacy. Charlotte was putting up a good front, but tension still bracketed her mouth. She had a lot more practice maneuvering through a media gauntlet than he did, but that didn't mean he wanted to subject her to one today. Thankfully, her security detail was on the same page, meeting them on the tarmac in an SUV.

"Is there a back entrance?" Noah asked the driver when he spied the throng of reporters camped outside the building housing the McManus penthouse.

"Already on it," the driver responded.

Charlotte squeezed his hand. "Still think I'm worth it?"

He answered her with a kiss, letting it linger despite their audience. She sighed into his mouth, only pulling back when the car came to a halt. They hurried inside and up to the penthouse.

The elevator doors opened to a spacious living room featuring a wall of windows overlooking the Inner Harbor. An animated movie was playing on the big screen television. Four little heads turned at the sound of the elevator.

"Aunt Charlie!" Two of the kids scrambled to their feet and ran into Charlotte's outstretched arms.

Noah watched as she sank into a nearby chair and pulled the twins into her lap.

"Oh, honey." Bridgette McManus wrapped her arms around Charlotte and her children.

Her husband stepped up behind the big chair, pulling the entire group into a giant hug. He kissed his sister on the head before his daughter demanded the same treatment. A hand landed on Noah's shoulder. He turned to find Brody Janik behind him. Brody's wife, Shay, was busy rounding up the other two kids.

"You good?" the tight end asked.

Noah nodded.

"Who wants to go swimming?" Brody's wife asked.

All four kids shouted out an ear-splitting "yes." The twins scrambled from Charlotte's lap, their excitement over seeing her forgotten in favor of a pool party with their cousins.

"Let's go get our suits on." Shay herded them to the other side of the penthouse.

"The network lawyers called while you were en route," McManus announced once the noise died down. "Kincaid was dismissed for cause before they came out of the commercial break. They are prepared to issue a written apology in all the major newspapers and social media sites tomorrow. I've asked them to run it through Bridgett beforehand."

"You have grounds for a major lawsuit, Charlie," Bridgett explained. "I don't want to let anyone off the hook that easily."

"I want to know how he found out," Charlotte said.

Bridgett sighed. "It seems the CEO we selected gets a little chatty after a few glasses of wine. Probably why her current company didn't match our offer to her. I hope I didn't overstep, but I withdrew our offer an hour ago."

Charlotte shook her head. "Of course I don't object."

McManus wrapped his arm around his sister. "You'll find

the right person. In the meantime, I'm going to cancel Bucky Kincaid so that he can't even get a job as a janitor in a professional sports locker room."

Noah cleared his throat. "If it's all the same to you, sir, I'll be looking after Charlotte's well-being from here on out. Kincaid is mine to deal with."

The air in the room stilled. Bridgett arched an eyebrow at him while her husband leveled a lethal look his way. Brody snickered. A muscle twitched in McManus' cheek. He shifted his eyes from Noah to his sister. Charlotte's smile was radiant as she gave him a half shrug.

McManus made an ugly sound before resettling his focus on Noah. "In that case, maybe we can dispense with you calling me 'sir.'"

"I've got a list of things I like to call him," Brody offered with a smirk.

"Brody!" The tight end's wife yelled from somewhere deep in the apartment. "You're supposed to be helping me with the kids!"

"I'm helping my teammate," Brody griped.

Bridgett rolled her eyes at her younger brother.

He sighed. "Tomorrow after film study." He gestured between himself and Noah. "I'll show you that list."

McManus made his way over to Noah and extended his hand. There was a twinkle in his eye Noah had never noticed before. "I put up with Brody because I love my wife. I suspect you'll be easier to tolerate."

Noah shook the other man's hand. Charlotte came up behind her brother, pulling both men in for an awkward hug. Noah was relieved when the elevator doors opened again, and McManus' personal assistant strolled out of it.

"Linc. Did you find anything?" Bridgett asked.

Linc's expression was glum. "It wasn't the pap we paid off

who leaked the photo. That guy's studio, including his photo storage, was incinerated in the wildfire that swept through Santa Rosa several years ago." He turned to Charlotte. "I'm sorry, Charlie. This one is on me."

Noah shifted closer to Charlotte.

"What are you talking about?" she demanded.

Linc pressed his fingers to his forehead. "Remember that law student I mentioned I was dating?"

Charlotte wiggled her eyebrows and smiled at Linc. "The one with all the moves?"

"Yeah." Linc groaned. "I found out last week she's actually a private investigator." Linc looked sheepish as he turned to his boss. "She was hired to conduct corporate espionage against McManus Industries."

The air in the room all but crackled.

"What are you saying?" McManus' tone was ominous.

His wife placed a calming hand on his chest. "Have you spoken to the company's security team?"

"Yes." Linc nodded. "They are the ones who caught her. Our firewall is impenetrable, so there's good news there. She didn't get anything. I already had a full briefing about this on your calendar for tomorrow."

"She somehow got the picture, though," Charlotte whispered.

Linc hung his head. "Yeah. It isn't kept in the company files for obvious reasons. I had it stored on a flash drive among a bunch of random ones locked in my desk. It was the only one that was labeled." He sighed. "It had your name on it, Charlie. I swear I only left her in my office for five minutes." He shook his head. "It was like leaving candy for a baby. Sorry doesn't even come close to how I feel right now."

A strained silence settled over the room. Linc pulled a

white envelope from his back pocket and held it out to McManus.

"I'll save you the trouble of firing me." He waved the envelope. "My letter of resignation."

"No!" Charlotte cried.

McManus avoided taking the envelope. "We'll discuss this tomorrow."

To everyone's surprise, Bridgett swooped in and plucked the envelope from Linc's fingers. "Resignation accepted."

Her husband and sister-in-law both donned stunned expressions.

"What do you think you're doing?" McManus asked.

Bridgett's smile bordered on diabolical. "I think I'm creating a win-win situation. Well, win-win for Linc and Charlotte. You, not so much." She turned to Charlotte. "You need a CEO. Someone, say, with an MBA from Wharton and tons of experience handling multiple companies." She pivoted to face a wide-eyed Linc. "And do you really want to be Jay's fixer forever?"

Linc's eyes darted between McManus and his wife. "Uh . . ."

"Hey, you can't steal him away from me like that," McManus argued.

"I've been trying to figure out a way to do this for weeks now," his wife replied. "It's the perfect solution. The investors all know him already. I may have already floated the idea to a few of them. They assured me they'll back off about taking Truly public if Linc comes on board. What do you say, Linc? Charlie?"

A slow grin spread over Charlotte's face. The tension that had gripped her mouth most of the day evaporated. "I can't think of anyone else I would rather work with."

Everyone looked at Linc. His conflicted expression relaxed into a slow grin. "I have so many ideas."

"Yay!" Charlotte threw her arms around Linc's shoulders. "And you won't make me feel like an idiot about any of it."

Linc laughed. "Girl, stop doubting yourself. You're brilliant. We are going to rock this."

Noah let out a relieved breath, thankful that Linc saw Charlotte for who and what she really was.

"Oh, don't pout," Bridgett cooed to her husband, who was indeed pouting.

"You're ruthless, you know," McManus grumbled.

She stretched up on her toes to kiss him. "You knew that when you married me." She patted his chest. "I'll make it up to you later. Now go take the twins to the pool. You don't want Brody teaching our children to swim. The man can barely float." She linked her arm through Charlotte's. "I found a children's book about surrogacy. Come see it before we all sit down with the kids tonight."

Bridgett led Charlotte over to the sofa.

McManus clapped Linc on the back. "Do I at least get two weeks' notice?"

Linc nodded. "I'm not really going anywhere." He gestured at Noah. "I have a feeling the incentive you were searching for to get Charlie to relocate is standing right here."

Charlotte's brother actually smiled. "Nothing could make me happier. Stay for dinner, both of you?"

Noah looked over at Charlotte, happier and more relaxed than he'd ever seen her. "Sure," he replied.

McManus nodded before heading off in the direction of the children's laughter.

"I've got a couple of TVs in my office downstairs," Linc said. "Wanna go check the scores?"

Noah nodded. "There's something I want to talk to you about while we're down there, as well."

———————

ONE WEEK LATER . . .

"They're ready for you, Noah." Asia stood at the entrance to the players only part of the locker room waiting to walk him into the press room.

"Don't forget to tell 'em how you put too much spin on that second touchdown pass, but I caught it anyway," Brody called out.

"Yeah, yeah," Noah replied.

Asia fell into step beside Noah as they walked down the narrow hall.

"I did give them all a not-so-gentle reminder to keep the presser from getting personal," she said. "You'd think that with another convincing win and three touchdown passes, that's what they'd want to talk to you about."

Jay McManus was leaning against the wall outside the media room when they rounded the corner.

"But no," Asia continued. "Once again, Bucky Kincaid inserts himself into the narrative." She shook her head. "The narcissist gets arrested for sexual misconduct and now women are coming forward, two a day, to tell their stories about him. Can you believe it?"

McManus locked eyes with Noah. "Kincaid's bad news," was all he said.

"For sure. I'll go in and remind them of the rules one more time." Asia slipped by them and into the room.

"Well done," McManus said.

"Thanks. It was a real team effort today."

"It was. But I was talking about Kincaid. That was very

well played. I thought my wife was fiendish, but even she's impressed. How did you do it, by the way?"

Noah shrugged. "Months after he started piling on me, people kept shooting me DM's, commiserating about him. Most were women. I was leery at first because I figured they might just want to get my attention." His jaw grew tight. "Too many of the stories were similar to the night I intercepted him with Charlotte. I kept a file with names and emails. I was waiting until I had enough evidence that Charlotte wouldn't have to stand up as one of the accusers. I wanted to keep her name out of it."

"Even when you weren't involved with my sister?"

Noah nodded.

McManus appeared to wrestle with his next words. "I was the first one to hold her when she was born. Her father was . . . somewhere else. He had been hoping for a son. She was sunshine and joy and for most of her life, I seemed to be the only one who noticed that about her." He met Noah's gaze. "Until you. At the risk of repeating myself, she's lucky to have you."

He opened the door and ushered Noah up to the podium. As usual, the room was a riot of noise, everyone with their hands in the air, jockeying for the first question. Noah called on the sideline reporter from Kincaid's former network.

"Bucky Kincaid had been badmouthing you for over a year now. Given recent events, is there anything you'd like to say to him today?" the guy asked.

Noah looked at the cameras lined up in the back of the room. The crowd squirmed in their seats, positioning their cellphones for the best shot.

"Yeah. Thanks for fixing me up with the woman I'm going to spend the rest of my life with."

I hope you enjoyed Charlotte and Noah's story. Wasn't it fun to catch up with the boys from the Baltimore Blaze? If you are like me, I'm always sorry to say goodbye to the characters in books. How about a bonus chapter? Scan the code and it's yours.

If you want more day to day details about my books, my crazy writing life, and opportunities to name places and characters, come hang out with my reader group, the X's and O's, on Facebook. Simply scan the code:

Are you curious about the other Baltimore Blaze players? You can read Shane Devlin's story in the one that started it all, **Game On.** Will Connelly has a fun secret baby story in **Foolish Games**. Brody Janik gets his HEA after a comical fake relationship in **Risky Game**. And of course, Charlotte is introduced in Jay and Bridgett's second chance romance, **Sleeping with the Enemy.**

How about more football? Meet the Milwaukee Growlers:
Just for Kicks – A marriage of convenience rom-com
Double Dog Dare – An enemies-to-lovers rom-com
Catch and Release — A second chance romance

And please, don't forget to tell other readers how much you enjoyed **Gossip Game** by leaving a review on the site where you purchased the book. It's the best way to show an author some love and I ALWAYS appreciate it!

How about a little suspense with your romance?

Recipe for Disaster – a mistaken identity Secret Service romance
Shot in the Dark – a forced proximity Secret Service romance
Between Love and Honor – a second chance Secret Service romance

Do you enjoy books about small towns and big families—including some sports stars? Check out my Chances Inlet series:

Back to Before – a forced proximity romance
All they Ever Wanted – an enemies-to-lovers romance
Second Chance Christmas – age gap romance
It Had to Be You – a nanny romance
Take Me Home for Christmas - a friends to lovers holiday romance

Go to TracySolheim.com to find out more about my books!

ACKNOWLEDGMENTS

In case you didn't notice, I based a few details in this book on real-life events. No, not the ones featuring a certain music icon and a football player—well, maybe one. Or two.

I'm talking about the zany auction to raise funds for the school. Years ago, the principal of our neighborhood elementary school "donated" a lunch where she'd dress as a bumble bee and chauffeur the kids in her fun ride—a yellow punch bug. I'm certain this wouldn't be allowed to happen in today's environment and really, it's too bad. It was wildly popular among the kiddos and parents got a little heated bidding on it. And, yes, there was a margarita machine at our auctions. Don't worry, the event wasn't held on school property!

The biggest coup of the night, however, was always the street sign. Scoring that bad boy for your student made mom and dad instant heroes. Alas, my husband and I were never heroes. We were too cheap to part with the thousands. Yes, I said thousands!

I hope you enjoyed the book. A big shoutout to Jeannie Moon for naming Truly Yours. Thank you to my beta readers, Jeannie, Melanie, Beth, and Kim for their insights. Mary Mullenbach, thank you for pitching in with a proofread. And, as always, a huge thank you to Rachael Brown for making sure the final version of Gossip Game was perfect. I couldn't do this without you, Rachael!

Thank you so much to everyone for taking the time to read my books. So many of you have become friends and, honestly, that is the greatest, and most unexpected, pleasure of this writing journey. Thanks to everyone for nagging me to finish Charlotte's story. It means the world to me that so many of you have stuck around since the first Baltimore Blaze book kicked off my writing career. It took me a while (ten years) to see her HEA, but I think Noah is perfect for her.

You guys are the best! Stick around. There are more stories to come.